"You like food, don't you?" Nick asked.

"No, I'm *obsessed* with food," she corrected him. "I have an understanding with God. He overlooks my gluttony, and I forgive Him for leaving me under-endowed on top."

Nick laughed, and was surprised by the sound. "He gave you enough to make you thoroughly dangerous," he said, letting his gaze drift over her face. "You're a beauty, Jenny."

"Not beauty," she said, shaking her head without being coy. "Just artfully arranged homeliness, but I kind of like it. My flaws are what make me me."

It wasn't pretense, he knew that instantly. She was wonderfully at ease with herself.

"I'm also known to be rebellious, I should warn you," she added.

"Why don't I find that surprising?" Nick said with a grin.

"I believe we were put on earth to make waves. So I make as many as I can," she finished wickedly.

He felt a sudden rush of excitement, and reached for her . . .

Bantam Books by Billie Green

WHAT ARE *LOVESWEPT* ROMANCES?

They are stories of true romance and touching emotion. We believe those two very important ingredients are constants in our highly sensual and very believable stories in the *LOVESWEPT* line. Our goal is to give you, the reader, stories of consistently high quality that may sometimes make you laugh, sometimes make you cry, but are always fresh and creative and contain many delightful surprises within their pages.

Most romance fans read an enormous number of books. Those they truly love, they keep. Others may be traded with friends and soon forgotten. We hope that each *LOVESWEPT* romance will be a treasure—a "keeper." We will always try to publish

LOVE STORIES YOU'LL NEVER FORGET
BY AUTHORS YOU'LL ALWAYS REMEMBER

The Editors

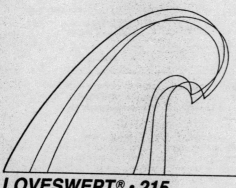

LOVESWEPT® • 215

Billie Green
Loving Jenny

BANTAM BOOKS
TORONTO • NEW YORK • LONDON • SYDNEY • AUCKLAND

LOVING JENNY

A Bantam Book / October 1987

If you would be interested in receiving protective vinyl
covers for your Loveswept books, please write to this address
for information:

Loveswept
Bantam Books
P.O. Box 985
Hicksville, NY 11802

ISBN 0-553-21844-1

Published simultaneously in the United States and Canada

PRINTED IN THE UNITED STATES OF AMERICA

O   0 9 8 7 6 5 4 3 2 1

One

It was a perfect day for a wedding. Spring had turned the gardens behind the Heywood mansion into a tastefully arranged explosion of color. Near the house a half acre of cemented pebbles surrounded a camelia-filled swimming pool. On a temporary platform to the left of the pool, an orchestra played, the faces of the white-tuxedoed musicians blurring into a solid entity, an entertainment machine.

Past the terrace, stone steps led down to a vast manicured lawn. The soft green of the grass made a gentle backdrop for the candy-striped pavilions that covered long tables of expertly displayed food. Between the tables, portable bars were judiciously placed so that no guest had to exert himself to reach a drink.

Unless one took the time to study them, the two hundred—odd guests were simply a mass of discreet colors. Celebrity watchers, however, could easily pick out a normally austere state senator laughing heartily at an ethnic joke told by a seven-foot basketball star; or the splashily dressed prince of a Middle Eastern country no one had ever heard of dancing with the queen of country and western music. To the tune of "Rhapsody in Blue" money mingled with power for the enjoyment of the less important guests, who hung excitedly on the fringe.

Ralph Heywood might have been born over a dry cleaning shop in a two-room apartment with apple crates for furniture, but by the time his only child made her much-touted entrance into the world, Ralph was well on his way to making his fifth or sixth million and the apple crates had given way to Sheraton and Hepplewhite.

Over the brim of a crystal champagne glass, Nick Reynolds's gaze passed over the glamour and power to watch his new bride dance with her father. The small blond woman's simple but elegant gown and her soft laughter were as effective as a sandwich board for letting everyone know that this was Elaine's turf, the kingdom her father had built for her.

Although Ralph Heywood's original company, Heywood Always Good Homestyle Pickles, was now one of his minor holdings, the title of Pickle King wouldn't die.

Not that Heywood minded, Nick thought, smiling slightly. Ralph was as proud of his humble beginnings as he was of his lovely daughter.

"I have seen the enemy and they are relatives."

Nick turned toward the voice and found Harold Edgy, his lawyer and best friend since high school, standing beside him. Nick grinned at his best man's rumpled appearance. Harry had a pretty-boy look that he fought diligently by wearing sloppy clothes and refusing to get a decent haircut.

"How many aunts and uncles does Elaine have, for heaven's sake?" Harry asked, his voice low, his eyes wary.

Nick laughed. "Ralph is an only child, but Elaine's mother was one of seven."

"Are they all patterned after Attila the Hun?"

"You must have met Uncle Edgar."

"Actually I think it was Aunt Virgie, but now that you mention it, she did have a rather attractive mustache." He took a hefty swig of imported champagne. "If you were determined to do it different this time, you succeeded beyond your wildest dreams."

"Are you trying to give me indigestion on my wedding day?" Nick asked, firming his lips to combat the twitch that always attacked the corner of his mouth when his ex-wife was mentioned.

Harry and his own wife, Sharon, had been the only guests to attend Nick's first wedding, an event Nick was trying very hard to forget.

"Sorry." Harry glanced at their surroundings with a jaundiced eye. "You can say a lot of stuff about Jenny, but when she was around, things were certainly never dull." He gestured with his glass toward the elegant crowd. "This shindig, my friend, is dull."

The twitch became more violent. It will pass, Nick assured himself. He had to give it time. Getting over the damage Jenny had done was like trying to clear away the effects of a nuclear disaster. It simply couldn't be done quickly.

"Not dull," he said. The effort to keep his voice

calm made him sound almost harsh. "Comfortable. Normal. Sane . . . thank heavens."

In an admittedly defensive move, he searched the crowd for Elaine. She was listening attentively to an elderly woman whose black dress and hat must have been new during Queen Victoria's reign. He was counting on Elaine to help complete the healing process. There were no strange twists and turns to his bride's mind. She was open, sweet, and slightly vulnerable, bringing out a latent protective instinct in him.

Jenny had never needed anything from him, he thought grimly, least of all protection. She had been tough enough to inflict devastating wounds, independent enough to walk out on him without looking back.

"Sane and dull are not mutually exclusive," Harry said, breaking the silence that had fallen between them. "I know Jenny caused a lot of trouble for you, but I can't help it—I like her."

"You didn't live with her."

"That's true," Harry agreed wistfully. "Sharon said I couldn't."

Nick grinned. Sharon Edgy was the least possessive person he had ever met. But then, there was no reason for her to be. Although Harry would deny it with his dying breath, he worshiped his wife.

For a moment Nick was tempted to tell Harry the reasons behind his second marriage. Still, while his agreement with Elaine seemed perfectly reasonable to him, he was afraid his friend wouldn't share that attitude. Harry didn't realize how rare was the love he and Sharon had found together. Harry had no reason to know that in ordinary married life, compromises were sometimes necessary.

Harry grinned at him. "I can't help comparing this to your last reception. Quite a contrast."

Nick nodded to one of Elaine's aunts—he couldn't remember which one—then looked at Harry. "Jenny and I didn't have a reception," he said, forcing calm into his voice. Knowing Harry, he would drop the subject whenever he achieved his objective and not a minute sooner.

"Sure you did." Harry was watching him from the corner of his eye. "Don't you remember that all-night diner?"

Against Nick's will, the memory brought a smile. The four of them had stopped at the little roadside diner after one in the morning. With the help of the two waitresses, the cook, and a truck driver, they had pushed back the tables to make a dance floor. He and Jenny had danced their wedding dance to the tune of "Mamas, Don't Let Your Babies Grow Up to Be Cowboys." Yes, he thought, this was quite a contrast.

"Those waitresses were gems," Harry said, his voice light with remembered pleasure. "Fabulous dancers, too . . . but not as good as Jenny. That old cook thought he was in heaven when he got Jenny to jitterbug with him. And remember the wedding cake? That was the best lemon pie I've ever had."

"Lord, yes," Nick said, chuckling as he was pulled into the memories against his will. "Meringue piled up to—" He broke off sharply, his fists clenching. "Cut it out, Harry. That was then; this is now. Jenny's a thousand miles away . . . and our marriage is even farther away than that. Can we leave off the stroll down memory lane?"

"A thousand miles . . ." Harry began, looking puzzled.

"I said I don't want to talk about her anymore." Nick's grim voice signaled the end of the conversation to anyone with discretion.

Harry had never been known for his discretion. "But, Nick, listen," he said urgently. "You've got it all wrong. Jenny—"

"See you later, Harry."

Without a backward glance Nick walked away. Almost immediately he knew he had overreacted. Harry was trying to prove a point, and Nick didn't doubt it was with the best of intentions. But the other man couldn't know of the countless painful, bewildered hours Nick had spent thinking of Jenny. He didn't want to think of her ever again.

He had made a wiser decision this time, he told himself as he moved through the crowd. This time would be different. No craziness, no soul-deep trauma.

He found Elaine by the buffet. Beside her, a thin elderly woman talked energetically. Luella Noble, Elaine's aunt, was a determined spinster and made sure everyone knew of her dislike of men.

"Miss Luella, do you mind if I steal Elaine for a few minutes?" Nick asked as he joined them.

"That's another thing, Elaine," the old woman said as though Nick hadn't spoken. "Men have absolutely no sense of family. They insist—"

"Glad you're enjoying the reception," Nick said pleasantly, and captured his bride's arm to gently but firmly escort her to the house. When they reached her father's study, he closed the door behind them.

"Aunt Lolly will never forgive you," Elaine said, smiling up at him.

"You've heard about her 'dreadful ordeal with the dentist' at least six times," he said as he pulled her into his arms. "I think you can wait a little longer for the seventh."

"Nicky," she protested, laughing softly as she eased herself from his arms and straightened her dress.

Elaine wasn't one for spontaneous affection, not like— Nick shut off the thought instantly. He didn't like the comparisons that entered his mind without his consent, especially when the comparisons leaned in Jenny's favor. He didn't want to remember that his ex-wife had her good points. If he had to think of Jenny, he would make it a rule to restrict his memories to the terrible scenes, the shouting matches.

No, even those memories had to be put behind him now. He had to concentrate on how calm life was around Elaine. No one could ever call Jenny calm. Marriage to her had been life on the edge, he thought grimly, unaware that it had taken only seconds for him to break his own rule.

"You're thinking about Jenny, aren't you?" Elaine asked, her voice filled with concern. "I can always tell by the look in your eyes. So much turbulence." She touched his shoulder. "She must have been awful."

He frowned. "In some ways she was the most caring person I've ever known," he said stiffly. Then, giving himself a mental shake, he relaxed.

"But I don't want to talk about Jenny. I'd rather talk about us and the future."

"It's perfectly reasonable that you should be thinking about Jenny today," Elaine persisted. "Present weddings always remind one of weddings in the past. Please don't think I mind. We made a bargain, remember? I want you to be able to talk to me about anything. In fact, it might be good therapy for you. You shouldn't keep it all locked up inside you."

Gawd, she's too good to be true.

The irreverent, Jenny-type remark jumped into his mind before he could control it.

Exasperated with himself, he shifted uncomfortably. Elaine smiled in understanding. "Don't worry about it, darling. I can wait. We have the rest of our lives for confidences."

The rest of our lives.

The words had a strange effect on Nick. They seemed to echo in the room, becoming more important with each repetition, until they were sharp points that jabbed at his mind and his heart.

Dammit, this was right, he told himself firmly. It had to be. He had screwed up once with Jenny. He couldn't afford to do it again.

Forcing his mind clear of all doubt, he exhaled slowly, then smiled as he took Elaine's arm. "Before we can get on with the rest of our lives, we have to get through this reception," he said, guiding her toward the door.

"Aren't you enjoying yourself?"

"What? Sure—I mean, of course I am," he said quickly. "Your father really pulled out all the stops."

Elaine laughed, obviously pleased with the reception. "That's because he likes you." She rubbed her cheek on his sleeve. "He totally approves of my choice."

As soon as they reached the patio, another of Elaine's aunts captured the bride to help resolve a family dispute. As the two women left him, Nick saw his mother heading in his direction. For a moment he considered ducking behind a potted palm, but decided it might look odd if the groom snubbed his own mother today of all days.

"Nicholas, dear," Mona Reynolds said as she reached him, "I must congratulate Ralph. This is a perfectly charming little get-together."

The blatant understatement had Nick stifling a sharp bark of laughter. From a blasé society matron, the offhanded compliment would sound unconscionably smug. Coming from his mother it bordered on the ridiculous.

Gazing down at her, he smiled wryly. In an unexplainable way, everything about Mona Reynolds was "too." Her clothes were too elegant, her hair too silvery perfect, her makeup too flawlessly discreet. She was too altogether right to be the real thing.

But then, could he view her objectively? Nick wondered. Somehow he was never able to look at his mother without seeing her as she had been when his father was alive, back when polyester print dresses and iron-gray home-permed hair were the norm.

Although Nick had never been very close to his parents, that had been his fault rather than theirs. Throughout his childhood Mona had been a loving mother and wife. When Nick's father died, though, her loneliness had brought out long-buried social-climbing tendencies, tendencies that at first amused then irritated her son.

The snobbishness had been unashamedly present in Mona's dealings with Nick's first wife. She had hated Jenny on sight and had tried in any way she could to get at her, sometimes resorting to petty, even childish tactics. Jenny, however, was no shrinking violet. She hadn't been the type to take even mild abuse lying down. Instead, she gave as good as she got. While Nick had to admit Jenny had been totally justified, it had certainly made for turbulent family relations.

When his marriage to Jenny had ended after three years, Mona had been obviously relieved. Her smug pleasure had become an irritant that caused him to avoid her as much as possible. Although he didn't like to admit it even to himself, the fact that his mother was so pleased with his marriage to Elaine aggravated the hell out of him. He had had his own reasons for proposing to Elaine, but his mother seemed to think she had engineered the whole thing.

"I spoke to Senator Aldridge about the garbage men," she was saying now, "and he agrees with me wholeheartedly. There is no reason for them to dress so tackily. Oh, and did you see me talking to Marisa Wynne? She was perfectly charming but a little on the dull-witted side, I'm afraid. Not at all what I expected of a princess. Lunch next week was mentioned, but I told her I would have to check my calendar." Mona glanced at a passing servant. "Would you look at his hair? It's impossible to get decent help these days. For heaven's sake, Nicholas, why couldn't you have had your morning coat made for you? These off-the-rack things look so—"

"Affordable?" he suggested dryly. "This suits me just fine, Ma."

"*Nicholas*," she hissed, glancing around in embarrassment, "how many times have I told you not to call me that? I know you do it just to annoy me, but for one day couldn't you consider my feelings and call me Mother?"

"Are you sure?" he asked. "Don't you think *Mater* has a more upper-crust ring to it?"

She rubbed her chin thoughtfully. "No . . . no, Mother will do just fine. *Mater* sounds a little pretentious."

He laughed, shaking his head. "We mustn't sound pretentious, must we?"

"Oh, look," she said, sending a frantic little wave over Nick's left shoulder. "There's the senator's wife. She promised to tell me where she got that perfectly charming little pearl brooch."

Freed of his mother's delightful company, Nick spent the next half hour wandering around the grounds, smiling until his teeth hurt, shaking hands with anyone who came near. He was muttering mysterious curses under his breath, when two of Elaine's uncles cornered him near a portable bar.

"Nick . . . listen Nick, we've been meaning to talk to you since you and Elaine started planning this thing, but you young people stay so busy we could never catch you."

"Yes, that's right," the other confirmed. "Never too late for advice."

Even though the two eldest Noble brothers were several years apart in age, Nick could never tell who was who. They always dressed in the same charcoal gray pinstripes and were shriveled to the same degree.

"Eugene, Dwight," he said, shaking hands with each as he hoped he never met the uncles separately. He wouldn't know which name to use. From what he had seen of them so far that didn't seem likely, though. They came as a pair. "What kind of advice did you have in mind?"

Eugene—or Dwight—cleared his throat. "It's of a somewhat intimate nature."

Nick hid his grin. "Intimate, you say?"

"Yes, that's right," Dwight—or Eugene—said, glancing around to make sure no delicate female ears were in eavesdropping range. "Intimate."

"The thing is, Nick, women are strange creatures—I'm speaking of women of Elaine's ilk, you understand. We men have to be careful of our . . . our baser natures when dealing with such women." The old man winked. "They don't understand some of the needs that men are cursed with."

Why the randy old coot, Nick thought, turning his startled laughter into a cough. "Is there something about Elaine's ilk that I should know?" he asked, his face solemn. "It was all right the last time I checked."

"No, no. You misunderstand. You see, my boy . . ."

As the two men began in turn to lecture him, Nick glanced around furtively. Where in hell was Harry when he needed him? He knew from experience these two old codgers could go on forever.

His gaze swept quickly over the area immediately around them, then stopped and retraced its path. Several yards behind Eugene and Dwight, the branches of a tall shrub, heavy with bright red flowers, began to move violently. Quirking one eyebrow in curiosity, Nick watched closely.

An earthquake? he mused, wondering if the

Cheech and Chong of the Geritol generation were beginning to affect his brain. An illicit meeting of lovers? An escaped gorilla, perhaps?

"And about excessive use of the tongue in kissing, Nick. What you should do . . ."

The pertinent advice was lost as Nick became mesmerized by the twitching bush. After a moment he saw a slender hand push aside some of the smaller branches near the top, and two large blue eyes appeared among the foliage.

". . . was the night I learned my lesson," Eugene—or Dwight—continued, stepping in front of Nick as though he sensed he was losing his audience.

Nick's palms began to tingle, and a twitch appeared at the corner of his mouth. Without thinking, he stepped toward the bush, leaving the two men staring after him.

As he drew nearer, the flowering branches parted briefly—just long enough for him to see the dark hair surrounding the thin, expressive face.

A wave of dizziness swept over him and was gone instantly. It couldn't be, he told himself forcefully. It was simply a trick of the imagination. Too much champagne. Too many memories.

But as he stared, the face disappeared and the hand appeared again, thumb up as it jerked in a smart-assed beckoning motion that was all too familiar to him.

Jenny.

Nick felt the shock rock through him in a violent explosion. Sensations, white-hot and heart-deep, left him momentarily paralyzed. It seemed he lived a dozen lifetimes in a few short seconds.

At last, forcing down the vivid, lightning-quick

emotions, he sought out one of them and concentrated on it with all his strength. Anger.

Diving through the shrubbery, he caught her by the arm. He didn't acknowledge her casual, "Hi, Nick," but jerked her around sharply and marched her toward a side door of the Heywood mansion.

A squeak was her only protest as they entered the house, and he pulled her down the hall toward the same room he and Elaine had used forty minutes earlier. After kicking the door shut behind them, he dropped her arm and stepped back, his movements uncharacteristically awkward.

It really was Jenny, he thought, his mind blurred with confusion and fury. Jenny, looking as though she had taken a quick trip to the store instead of having disappeared for two years. How could she still look the same?

As she stood motionless, waiting for him to make the next move, Nick pulled up all the objectivity he could muster to study her, hoping the time would calm the savage beating of his heart.

Her hair was as black as his but with hidden lights that seemed to dance around her face. It was smooth, turning under to brush her slender shoulders, and the sides and top were swept back carelessly. Her brilliant blue eyes were large, giving her the deceptive look of an innocent, inquisitive child. The long legs, the small breasts, the tender mouth, were as familiar to him as his reflection in a mirror.

It was all the same . . . and it was totally different. The unique silent communication that had always connected their minds wasn't there. The gleam of love that had been in her eyes only for him had disappeared without a trace.

The Jenny he had once loved was gone and this beautiful stranger with the distant eyes had taken her place.

Why, when he was finally getting his life straightened out, had she come back to mess it up? She might be a virtual stranger, but he still recognized the set of her stubborn chin. Trouble.

"All right, I'm calm now, Jenny," he said, his breathing slow and careful. "Why, when you're supposed to be in San Francisco—a safe distance, I thought—are you here? And for sweet heaven's sake, why did you choose today?"

"If you get any calmer, you'll bust an artery," she said, her eyes sparkling. "As incredible as it sounds, I don't think you're glad to see me."

His laugh was sharp and angry. "Ask me if I would be glad to see a hurricane . . . a great white shark . . . fire, famine, or flood. Ask me how I'd like having Typhoid Mary to dinner some night."

"I missed you too," she said, grinning. "That's some party you've got going out there. The little pickle heiress sure knows how to throw a wedding."

"Jenny," he said, his voice tight with warning.

"I wish I had seen the wedding," she continued blithely, as though unaware of his fury. "Of course, I read about it in all the newspapers. VIPs flying in from all over the country. Caterers and florists preparing for months. The bride's dress will probably be as famous as Princess Di's." She paused thoughtfully. "No, with those hips, it would have to be Fergie's dress."

"Dammit, Jenny," he said with barely subdued force, "tell me why you're here. Tell me why you felt it necessary to disrupt my wedding reception." He paused, a dangerous gleam in his eye.

"If this is one of your games, you can pack it up and go home. I will not have you upsetting Elaine."

She stared at him, some secret, suppressed emotion glinting in her eye and making him wary. "I'm afraid we might not be able to avoid doing that, ex-o'-mine," she said softly.

He inhaled slowly, his hands tingling wildly with the need to do her bodily harm. "No more prevarication, Jenny. Just tell me what's going on."

"You're not going to like it."

The laughter in her voice made him grind his teeth. *"Tell me."*

Moving away from him, she slid onto Ralph Heywood's huge mahoghany desk and rested her chin on slender fists as she studied his stony expression. "Do you ever watch *Twenty/Twenty*?" she asked finally.

"What does that have to do with anything? I don't have time for—"

"I'm getting there," she said, interrupting his tirade. "This week's show was preempted locally because of that manhunt up in Denton. They aired it today—just a couple of hours ago." She raked a hand through her silky hair, and Nick could tell she was stalling. "I must say it was one of their better efforts. First they showed a segment on women executives in the automobile industry. You wouldn't believe what those women have to put up with— Okay, okay. Keep your pants on," she said hastily as he stepped closer. "The second feature was an exposé of a Mexican divorce scam."

Nick felt his heart jerk. His features grew unnaturally still as he fixed his unwavering gaze on her. "Go on," he said smoothly.

She shifted her own gaze to the ceiling. "It seems this lawyer, Jesus Escobar, wasn't really a lawyer at all. He would ask his client for a large advance to 'grease the wheels of bureaucracy,' then he would produce fake divorce papers." She smiled, but it was a small, nervous gesture. "Isn't that a kick? He had a great thing going for a while. They said he swindled hundreds of American couples."

Nick felt every nerve, every muscle stretch so tightly they burned. "What was your lawyer's name, Jenny?" He knew the low, tense words sounded threatening. He knew and he didn't care.

She slid agilely from the desk and backed away steadily, her breath catching in a hesitant laugh. "I love the way your mouth twitches like that," she said, then squeaked when he grabbed her arm.

"My lawyer's name? As a matter of fact, it was Jesus Escobar," she said, moistening her lips. "How's that for a weird coincidence? Nick . . . Nick, stop. You're cutting off the circulation in my arm."

He released her and stared at her glassily. "Are you trying to tell me—"

She raised her hands in a helpless gesture. "I'm afraid so. The divorce wasn't legal." She looked up at him through her long dark lashes, her smile that of an innocent child. "We're still married, Nick."

Two

Jenny watched Nick's stunned face as the unexpected information sunk in. It had taken all her effort to keep this scene light. Melodrama was just exactly what she didn't need. But the tight hold she had placed on her emotions threatened to slip.

Now that she was actually with him it was difficult for her to pretend she felt nothing. Hundreds of emotions were warring for supremacy. But there was only one she allowed herself to think of now—how strange it felt to be near him with no love between them.

It was as though the world were slightly off kilter, as though she were in another dimension. Added to that, she felt the same kind of nostalgic pain that one associated with the death of a loved one.

Nick had changed visibly in the two years they had been apart. His thick black hair still showed no hint of gray, and it was still as uncompromisingly straight as his back. But the lines around his mouth and eyes seemed deeper. His naturally dark skin, inherited from a long-forgotten Latin ancestor, seemed more taut but less vital. The regal shape of his nose and cheekbones—always at odds with his square, stubborn jaw—seemed more sharply defined. Jenny had always thought the Architect must have had a specific design in mind then changed His mind at the last minute just for the hell of it.

If anything had remained exactly the same, it was Nick's eyes. They were an ordinary shade of brown until those rare occasions when he lost his temper, then they flamed with sable fire. They were flaming now.

Holding her breath, she waited for the explosion she knew from experience was coming. She was right.

"Good God almighty!" he shouted, swinging around with clenched fists. "How could you? Even you couldn't be so careless. If you're making this up, Jenny, so help me I'll wring your neck." He inhaled deeply. "Why now? Why not before the wedding?"

"I came as soon as I knew. But it was too late; you were already a—" She paused, struggling to keep a straight face. "You were already a bigamist."

"It's not funny, damn you!" he exploded.

"I know, I know." She shook her head, sobering quickly. "I didn't plan it this way . . . honest, Nick. I thought he was legitimate. Well, I ask you, how can you not trust a man named Jesus?"

She stepped closer, unwilling sympathy showing in her blue eyes. "It's a terrible thing to have happen, especially now. But it can be fixed. I'll simply get another divorce, and no one will ever know. You don't even have to tell the bride if you don't want to."

He closed his eyes. "You're talking as if the recipe for a cake didn't turn out quite right so you've decided to make another one. It's not that simple. If the divorce isn't legal, then the wedding today isn't either. We'll have to do it all over again."

"Then you may have to tell her," Jenny admitted prosaically.

Ignoring the comment, Nick stared at her as though she were an unpadded vial of nitroglycerin. "You did this on purpose, didn't you?"

Jenny's eyes widened in disbelief. "That's crazy."

He began to pace back and forth in front of the desk. "You thought, Old Nick is getting a little too comfortable; his life is just a little too sane. Now, how can I shake him up a little?"

"Why should I do it on purpose?"

He stopped walking to glare at her. "How in hell should I know? Have I ever understood the way your mind works? Why did you set my office on fire? And—"

"That was an accident!"

"—why did you invite fifty people over to watch me take a bath?"

"That was to show off the tub I got you for your birthday. You loved that tub. Besides, you thought the whole thing was hilarious," she accused hotly. "You had Sharon and Harry roaring when you made a soap-bubble goatee."

This information didn't seem to please him. When he looked as though he was about to continue the list of her sins, she held up a restraining hand. "You're being paranoid. If you'll calm down, you'll see this doesn't make sense. The divorce was my idea—why would I deliberately screw it up?"

"To irritate me," he said, rubbing the back of his neck as though it ached. "That's all the excuse you ever needed." Exhaling roughly, he sat on the desk beside her. "Hell, Jenny, how am I going to tell Elaine?" He groaned. "And her family? You saw that circus out there. How am I going to tell them it didn't count?"

"Just tell them," she said in a soothing voice as she began to massage the taut muscles in his neck. "They'll understand. From what I hear, Heywood thinks you're the catch of the year." Feeling the warmth of his flesh under her fingers, Jenny suddenly realized what she was doing and jerked her hand away. Shifting to put some distance between them, her voice became sharper. "As for the guests, it's none of their business. They don't have to know that you're going to redo the ceremony later. In fact, no one has to know except the bride."

When he simply stared into space, she sighed. "Oh, for heaven's sake, stop looking so tragic. I assume the little heiress loves you; she married you. She'll understand that it wasn't your fault."

"Elaine will understand," he said wearily as he stood and walked away from the desk. "And maybe even her father will understand . . . eventually. But her uncle Edgar will have my balls on a platter. He can't stand the sight of me—and he's a judge, no less. It would give him the thrill of his life to have me brought up before him on bigamy charges."

Right on cue, the door opened and a man

stepped into the room. He was probably in his sixties, but his figure was trim and he looked strong. Wiry gray hair that shone like polished steel was cropped close to his head. The granite-like face gave a clue to his personality. Here was a man who saw black and white, right and wrong, and never made allowances for human frailty.

Jenny slid off the desk as the man stepped closer.

"Edgar," Nick said. Only someone who knew Nick as well as Jenny could have picked up on the wariness in his voice. "This is Jenny. . . ."

As Nick paused, Jenny jumped into the breach. "Jenny Valiant." When she offered him her hand, the older man shook it reluctantly. From the old school, she thought. He was obviously a Southern gentleman who thought only men shook hands while women simpered in the background.

"I use my maiden name," she continued, "and it always throws Nick off balance. You know what a male chauvinist he is." The older man's expression was unyielding. After running her gaze over him slowly, she met his eyes. "West Point?"

Immediately his features softened in surprise. "Why, yes. How did you know?"

She smiled. "I don't know, there's just something about an army man. An inner strength and control."

His gaze slid over her jeans and sweatshirt. "You're a guest?"

She laughed. "No, I'm not that liberated." She glanced down at her gray sweatshirt and faded jeans. "This is my wedding-crashing outfit."

"She's an old friend," Nick interjected hastily.

"Since she's in town only for the day, she decided to drop by to . . . to congratulate me."

Uncle Edgar apparently still had his doubts. He glanced from Jenny to Nick. "Has Elaine met her?"

Jenny bit her lip to keep from laughing. The old man had put a wealth of feeling into the word *her.* It was just one syllable, but the word was easily interpreted as "this person who is obviously the wrong sort, maybe even a woman of loose morals, or she wouldn't be hiding in the study with this man that I really don't care for and would have stopped my niece from marrying if I could have done it discreetly."

"No," Nick said calmly. "Jenny didn't want me to take Elaine away from the reception."

Nick was no longer playing the old man's game. Jenny could have told Uncle Edgar about how difficult it was to intimidate someone like Nick. He was a man who could be pushed only so far.

"That was thoughtful of her," Uncle Edgar said stiffly. "But a bride needs her groom beside her at her wedding reception." As though he realized he had gone too far, the older man cleared his throat. "I'd better get back myself." He glanced reluctantly at Jenny. "Nice meeting you, Miss . . . ahem . . . Miss—"

"Valiant," she supplied. "And the pleasure was all mine, believe me." As he walked out, she saluted the closing door, then turned to Nick. "I assume old blood-and-guts is his honor your uncle-in-law."

He nodded. "He'll massacre me," he said, his voice fatalistic.

"Why don't you fix him up with your mother?"

Jenny said, her eyes sparkling with wicked humor. "I'd give her a week to whip him into shape."

Nick stared at her for a moment, then burst out laughing. The sound caused a deep warmth to grow inside Jenny, the kind of warmth she had forgotten was possible.

"Damn, I ought to do just that," Nick said, still chuckling. "Remember that Greek car salesman?"

The memory brought a gurgle of laughter from her. "That poor man. He strode in a conquering Greek hero and slunk out worried that his shoelaces were tied wrong. She even had him convinced his accent was in bad taste."

As she spoke, Nick ran his gaze over her face, dwelling on the sparkling blue eyes. "How long have you been using your maiden name?" he asked, his voice carefully controlled.

She glanced away. "Just since I got back to Fort Worth two months ago," she said, shrugging casually. "I figured it would be better that way."

"Two months?" he asked, his expression becoming remote again. "You've been in town for two months and I didn't know about it."

Before she could respond, he moved away from her and the empathy that had been growing between them faded.

"We've got decisions to make." His voice was harsh now. "We've got to find the quickest way to get this thing over with once and for all."

This thing, she thought dully. She wanted to say, Hey buster, this is my life you're talking about; show a little respect. But she didn't. Jenny knew he had every right to be annoyed.

At that moment the door opened again. Jenny

threw up her hands. "What is this—Grand Central Station?" she muttered helplessly.

The woman who walked in was a small, lushly built blonde. Jenny didn't need the white satin wedding dress to tell her this was the bride.

"Nicky?" the woman said softly. "Uncle Edgar said—" she broke off, shifting her gaze to Jenny, and smiled politely. "Hello. I don't believe we've met. I'm Elaine Heywood—no, that's not right," she said, laughing softly. "I'm Elaine Reynolds."

"That's what you think," Jenny muttered under her breath.

"Aren't you going to introduce us?" the bride asked Nick, then she grew still as she examined his eyes. Turning back to Jenny, she said hesitantly, "Jenny?"

"The one and only," Jenny said, her voice bright. Moving back to the desk, she hopped up and settled down to view the scene with uninhibited interest.

Elaine turned back to Nick. "Something's wrong. What is it?"

He put a protective arm around her shoulder. "Don't look so worried, darling," he said gently. "You're right. It is bad news, and you're going to have to be brave."

Jenny rolled her eyes, then immediately assumed a bland expression when Nick glared at her.

"What is it, Nicky?" Elaine asked, her voice trembling slightly.

"Elaine . . . we have a problem, darling. Jenny found out today that the Mexican lawyer she hired to handle our divorce was a phony."

Elaine glanced at Jenny. "How terrible for you. I

hate it when people are dishonest. It makes one feel so stupid."

"It makes one feel more than that," Jenny said wryly. "Sometimes it makes one feel positively attached."

Elaine's smile was hesitant, her gaze confused. "I'm sorry. I'm not too bright on legal matters. Are you going to sue? If you need any advice, I'm sure Uncle Edgar would be happy to help."

When Nick shifted in discomfort, Jenny couldn't tell if it was caused by the situation or his new bride's denseness.

"I'm afraid it's not just Jenny's problem," Nick said. "You know what this means, don't you?"

She frowned. "It means she was cheated."

Jenny swallowed her startled laughter and kept her expression bland.

"The divorce is not legal."

Elaine frowned, her smooth brow wrinkling in concentration. "And our marriage?" she asked hesitantly.

Jenny looked at the ceiling. "And the little lady wins the ceramic dalmatian and a trip to Las Vegas," she murmured, confident that neither of them was paying the slightest attention to her.

"I'm afraid our marriage isn't legal either."

Elaine swayed slightly, closing her eyes, then made a visible effort to get a grip on herself. Observing the scene, Jenny felt reluctant sympathy for the woman. If she were being totally objective, she would say Elaine's problem was not a lack of intelligence, but simply the result of having been pampered and protected all her life. If things have always gone right, it is difficult to understand when they go wrong. Of course, Jenny would only say that if she were being totally objective, and she wasn't.

After a long moment Elaine smiled up at Nick. "I trust you, Nicky. I know you'll work it out." She bit her lip. "Do we have to tell everyone? Father . . . Uncle Edgar?"

"Hell no," he said emphatically, then caught himself and said in gentler tones, "no, I promise no one will have to know. I'll take care of it"—he glanced at Jenny—"and this time it will be legal. Now, why don't you go back to the reception. I'll join you in a few minutes."

"Shouldn't I be with you?"

"No, this problem is none of your doing. I'll handle it. You'd better take care of our guests."

"Yes, I suppose you're right." At the door she paused, giving Jenny a puzzled glance. Then she walked out.

Jenny watched as the door closed behind Elaine. "Not real quick, is she?"

Nick jerked his head around, glaring at her with ice cold anger.

"I shouldn't have said that," she said, sighing with regret as she slid from the desk. "As a matter of fact, I suppose I even admire her. She could have made a real doozie of a scene. I guess what's bothering me is"—she examined his face with genuine bewilderment—"is that really the kind of woman you want?"

"Yes," he said. His voice was a little too loud, his tone a shade too emphatic. "A quick wit may be a plus in advertising, but it can be a definite drawback in marriage."

His accusation hurt, but when Jenny remembered all the cutting, hurtful things she had said to him in anger, she silently acknowledged her culpability.

Nick turned away, allowing her a view of his stiff shoulders. "Elaine doesn't pull stupid stunts and she doesn't have a temper. She has never once locked me out of the house in freezing cold weather, and she has never dumped minestrone on a business associate."

"It was vichyssoise, and he deserved it. I wish it had been hot." Jenny's hurt turned to fury. While she admitted she had made mistakes in their marriage, he had no right to beat her with them now.

"Yes, I can see that the bride wouldn't rock the boat," she said, smiling sweetly as she tried to keep her voice steady. "She looks very . . . placid. Tell me 'Nicky darling,' how can you tell when she's awake and when she's asleep?"

Nick's face tightened, red spots defining his cheekbones as he stepped toward her. "Damn you—"

Jenny raised her chin belligerently and met his blazing gaze with one of her own. For several seconds they merely glared, each waiting for the other to break first.

"Oh, hell," she said roughly, raking a hand through her hair. "Okay, I'm sorry—I'm *sorry,*" she whispered, angry with herself. "I wouldn't have insulted the bride if you hadn't tried to get at me. I had forgotten how quickly you can make me lose my temper."

"I don't even have a temper when I'm not around you," he said, then exhaled in a harsh breath. "Yes . . . I'm sorry too. It doesn't help anything for us to be at each other's throats like this."

"Right," she said perfunctorily, "now that we've established that we still hate each other, what are we going to do about this mess?"

"Hell if I know." He shook his head wearily. "I need time to think. And I still have to get through the reception. We're supposed to stay at the Hilton tonight then leave for France tomorrow." He ran his hand across his jaw. "Damn, I hate putting it off, but I can't ask Elaine to go on our honeymoon until we're legally married."

His concern for Elaine was beginning to irritate her. "Well, of course you can't," she said in mock sympathy. "Princesses must have unencumbered princes."

Before he could explode again, Jenny headed for the door. She paused with her hand on the knob and looked back. "Nick," she said quietly, "I really am sorry. I never intended to cause you any more trouble."

For one brief second something flared in his eyes, something exciting, something that took her back to other days, other emotions. Then the brightness was gone and his expression was coldly polite as he nodded.

Jenny exhaled slowly and walked out.

Three

Nick watched in stony silence as the door closed behind Jenny. For several minutes he held his stiff pose, his fists clenched at his sides. He clenched them to keep from slamming them into the wall.

When he was positive she was not coming back, Nick began to pace, his movements mechanical. He felt as though someone had put a cattle prod to his raw nerves. She had always been able to do this to him, damn her. Being around Jenny made him feel wired. Sweet heaven, he thought, inhaling roughly, she made him feel alive.

Jenny, damn her soul. Jenny—once the love of his life. Jenny—for two years an empty space in his heart. Jenny—who'd left behind agonizing nights, interminable days, and irreparable wounds.

In the past two years, during countless sleepless nights, he had carefully examined the pain of loving Jenny. He had relived every moment, every argument, every hurtful word that had flown between them, torturing himself again and again with the memories until he had become emotionally anesthetized.

But there were things he had chosen to forget during those nights, things he had had to forget for the sake of his sanity. He had blocked out the image of how vital, how real Jenny was. He had shut out her beauty, beauty so achingly poignant that it made him catch his breath.

Not beauty, just artfully arranged homeliness.

Jenny had made the disclaimer the first time he had ever seen her. The memory always had the power to make him smile, as he was reluctantly smiling now.

It was six years ago, on a diamond-bright spring Sunday that he had arrived at his boat slip on Lake Worth later than usual. Business calls kept getting in his way, causing him to feel a deeper tension than normal.

Since he had held his position as president of EDH Enterprises for only two years, Nick was still considered new kid on the block, but things were gradually changing for him at the company. He was making it his job to see that they did.

EDH owned, among other things, two restaurant chains and a fast-growing line of specialty foods. After a long period of slow growth, the company had finally come into its own and was expanding rapidly, creating rising interest in the business world. When the board of directors had first appointed him president, Nick knew what they had in mind for him. Certain members of the board wanted a puppet to carry out their orders.

However, in choosing Nick they had made a serious mistake. He was no man's pawn. Consequently, the first eighteen months had been no more than a series of head-on collisions between him and the board. It was only recently that they had finally begun to accept the fact that the man they had chosen would do only what he considered was right for the company. And at that point Nick had too many of the major stockholders backing him for the board to do anything about it.

Occasionally, on days such as this particular Sunday, one of the members of what Nick secretly termed the loyal opposition would try to throw a spanner into the works. Then it took all his ingenuity to overcome the crisis. Although Nick thrived on the business, the constant hassle was sometimes physically and mentally draining.

His small sailboat was the one place Nick could leave business behind and truly unwind. On his boat he was completely isolated. No telephones. No newspapers. No radio. Just the water, the wind, and the blue sky God had seen fit to lend to Texas.

Using the auxiliary motor, he carefully pulled the *Reunion* away from the wooden dock. Out in open water, he killed the motor and began the job of raising the sails. Every move had been made hundreds of times before, and the routine had become part of the enjoyment.

It was only on Sundays that Nick could shut off the hurtling speed of his brain. There was no thought on Sunday, only instinct and a gentle peace. He had made it a rule never to have guests on the *Reunion*. That, too, was part of the routine. To ask Harry or one of the women he occasionally dated along would turn his day into nothing more than a Sunday outing. It would take away the depth, the meaning of the whole experience. He couldn't think of a single person whom he would not consider an intruder on this time.

Stooping to untangle a line, Nick mentally began to abandon the world. He supposed he really was the detached son of a bitch Harry often called him. The detachment wasn't something he had learned. There was no traumatic experience in his background to make him view other members of his species from a distance. It had been a part of his character for as long as he could remember.

As a young boy he had, like all other children, longed to be less isolated. Life without personal connections had been lonely. But as he matured he had learned to live with and eventually accept his difference. He still had difficulty understanding the emotional loops that ruled and sometimes ruined other people's lives. To him, it seemed an irrational, disorganized way to live.

Nick stood straight and tall, grasping a nylon line as he looked out over the water and the sky, each a blue so bright it hurt the eyes. Willingly, he began to free himself of all thought. He didn't merely push reality to a corner of his brain; in a process not even he understood fully, he disposed of it completely.

For this one day of the week he wasn't Nicholas Reynolds, president of EDH Enterprises, Inc.; he was simply another component of that complex organism, the Earth. He was a part of the water and the wind.

"You look like Leif Ericson discovering a new world."

At first the words barely penetrated Nick's consciousness, then he frowned as they nudged and poked and finally broke through. He swung around as the voice went on.

"I've always wondered if old Leif really liked exploring, or if he was simply trying to find a place where the neighbors wouldn't come knocking at his door every Saturday to borrow the lawn mower."

The owner of the voice was sitting cross-legged on the deck behind him, speaking as though she were continuing a conversation begun earlier. At that point Nick didn't take in the particular details of her appearance. He merely had the vague impression that her looks were striking and clear-cut. The fact that she was on his boat, where no one was supposed to be, took all his concentration.

"Where in hell did you come from?" he asked harshly.

Shifting her position, she wrapped her arms around long legs left bare by tight white shorts and smiled. "I'm a stowaway."

"Yes, I can see that," he said, shaking away the prevarication with an irritated jerk of his head. "That tells me absolutely nothing. Who are you? And why are you here, on my boat?"

"I'm Jenny Valiant." As she spoke, her gaze drifted over him, examining him carefully. "If the name sounds familiar, it's because I've given it to your secretary at least a dozen times in the past two weeks. Don't you ever return your calls? I know Fowler's is smaller than the advertising agency you've been using, but we're also hands-down better. Who on earth talked you into that idiotic 'real people' campaign for your chain of steakhouses?" she asked, her tone openly pitying. "We could top that without even bringing out the big mental guns."

"You trespassed and invaded my privacy to talk about advertising?" He fought an overwhelming urge to pick her up and throw her overboard. "If you have to use this sort of overbearing tactic, why aren't you using it on the EDH publicity people?"

She shrugged. "I've tried that. They said you chose the firm that does your advertising. Any change would have to come from you."

As a matter of fact, Nick had not been satisfied with the advertising that had been done for the Boar and Hound chain. But asking him to think about it now was too much. This was *his* time, dammit.

"You know," she said quietly, as though sensing his mood, "if you'd just check out some of the things we've done, you'll see that we do only top-notch work. I can get a list to you first thing Monday morning, or, better yet, I can bring some videos to your office."

He stared at her silently for a long, drawn-out moment. Belatedly he noticed the wide-spaced blue eyes that rivaled the spring sky in clarity, the full, sensuous lips, the sleek lines of her body.

"I never talk business on Sunday," he said

abruptly. If his voice was just a little more harsh than the situation warranted, it was because he resented the pleasure he found in simply looking at her.

Turning away, he began to pull on the rope that would raise the mainsail. "Go aft and raise the other sail. Secure it just like I'm doing with this one."

Afterward Nick could never pinpoint the exact moment he had decided not to take her back to the docks. He didn't even know if the decision had been one he had made consciously. Perhaps from the very beginning there had been no alternative to loving Jenny.

The next few hours could have been played in a series of vibrant still shots. Jenny, her dark hair whipping around her face. Jenny, laughing in innocent delight at the foolish antics of the gulls. Jenny, her face intense with concentration as she learned to help him sail the *Reunion*. Jenny, moving beside him as though she belonged there.

They spoke rarely, saying only what was absolutely necessary. She made mistakes in helping him, but she refused to give up, trying again and again until she got it right.

Once, late in the morning, Nick pulled back and tried to recapture his initial irritation. He tried to bring back the feeling that she was an intruder. When he couldn't, he didn't try again. He didn't want to examine why being with this woman suddenly felt right. Not today. Sunday wasn't for thinking. Sunday was for feeling.

In early afternoon he anchored the boat in a small, isolated cove. Retrieving a wicker basket from belowdeck, he sat down and pulled out a bottle of wine. After uncorking the wine, he poured a single glass, then brought out a wrapped sandwich and a plastic dish of potato salad.

Leaning against the rail, Jenny watched as he took the first bite. "I'm really not hungry," she said haughtily, ignoring the loud protest of her stomach.

Nick hid a smile. Casually reaching in the basket, he pulled out another sandwich and tossed it to her. She stretched eagerly to catch it. Then, grinning her thanks, she moved closer to him. Within five minutes they were sharing the potato salad and drinking from the same glass as though they were lifelong companions. He found that Jenny Valiant was no delicate flower where food was concerned. She ate with obvious, almost sensual relish.

"You like food," he said, handing her the wine-glass.

"No, I am obsessed with food," she corrected him, sipping the wine. "But I have an understanding with God. He overlooks my gluttony, and I forgive Him for short-sheeting me in the breast department."

He laughed and was surprised by the sound. "He gave you enough to make you thoroughly dangerous," he said, letting his gaze drift over her face. "In fact, I'm surprised that while I was taking in the beauty all around me, I overlooked the beauty here in my own boat."

"Not beauty," she said, shaking her head without a hint of coyness. "Just artfully arranged homeliness. Not exactly magazine-cover material, but I kind of like it. The flaws are what make me me."

It wasn't a pretense. Somehow Nick knew that she was totally at ease with her physical self. It was something he had rarely seen in a man and had never encountered in a woman. In his experience, women—young or old—were either outright vain about their looks or obsessed by some imperfection, no matter how minor.

"You're looking at me in a strange kind of way," she said, tilting her head to the side. "If you wanted the last of the potato salad, you should have spoken sooner." She held up the empty carton. "I killed it."

"I'm glad you liked it," he said politely. His eyes sparkled with amusement.

"I'm a pig," she said contentedly as she repacked the basket. "One of my many faults. I'm also—according to my boss and my pastor—rebellious."

"Why do I find that totally unsurprising?"

She grinned. "I firmly believe we were put on this earth to make waves. So I make as many as I can," she added wickedly, then raised her face to the sun in a gesture resembling pagan worship.

He shook his head, laughing again as he stretched out full length on the deck. Resting his head on his hands, he stared up at the sky. The easy laughter was another thing he wouldn't question today, he decided. Staring sightlessly overhead, he let the rays of the sun cover him, absorbing the warmth as it sank into his body and reached his core.

Five jets flying in formation intersected his line of vision. He briefly allowed them into his consciousness, then they were gone.

"What are they doing?"

He glanced at Jenny. She was leaning lazily against the rail again as she watched the planes disappear. "They're heading for the Air Force base to conduct a mock bombing raid for the public," he said.

She choked on the wine, then laughed in surprise. "What will they do for an encore—a mock mass execution?"

He chuckled deep in his throat. "Pack a picnic lunch and bring the kiddies."

Nick sensed rather than saw her smile as she put down the wineglass and moved to lie beside him, sharing his view of the sky.

"Lord, I love people," she said with real feeling in her voice. "There's no logic to them. Every time you turn around they're doing something crazy or shocking, and sometimes they're doing something so wonderful that it makes you want to cry. I don't think if I lived a million years I would ever figure them out."

Nick had rolled onto his side to watch in growing, somewhat reluctant fascination as she spoke. After studying her clean-cut, vital features for a few moments, he said in surprise, "You really do enjoy it, don't you? The inconsistency, the irrationality."

She glanced at him. "Don't you? No, I supposed you don't." Her eyes held, not pity, but something totally surprising. It was warm, almost loving sympathy. "You have a kind of unyielding strength," she said slowly. "I think you've probably learned to tolerate the human condition. I'm excited by it. So much so that I usually jump in with both feet. I'm impulsive, but consciously so—if that makes any sense. I gave myself permission to be just as wacky as the rest of the human race. You observe life; I wallow in it."

There was a painful tightening in his chest as he let her words sink in. This woman was too vivacious, too alive to have experienced the same remoteness that had afflicted Nick all his life. Unreasonably, he felt almost as bereft in his separateness as he had in childhood.

"Can I tell you something that might shock you?" Her voice was as gentle as her eyes.

He stared at her for a moment in silence. He felt he was on the verge of something, although he couldn't tell what. The palms of his hands tingled in a strange, uncomfortable way. After a moment he nodded, uncertain whether he wanted to experience this or not.

"You're one of us, Nick."

"I beg your pardon," he said. Once again she had surprised him. "I'm one of who?"

She laughed softly. "You sit and watch and shake your head at the world, wondering how it can survive when it's so screwy. You see the grown man who has to have his lucky nickel in his pocket before he makes a business deal, or the woman who works her butt off all day then goes home to pamper a man only God could love. You see all these things and can't identify with the irrationality."

His eyes narrowed, effectively admitting she had scored a direct hit.

"Yes, I thought so," she said, nodding. "But you're overlooking something. Every Sunday you come here to sail alone—the people at the marina gave me that information. And I'll bet that you park your car in exactly the same spot every morning and keep your underwear in exactly the same drawer and ask for exactly the same amount of starch in your shirts each time. You love this boat and feel deeply about the experience of being out here alone with nature—I can see that in your face and your eyes."

"So," he said stiffly.

"So," she said, raising her head to rest it on her hand as she looked up at him. "You have foibles, Nick. They're orderly, methodical foibles, but they're still foibles. Just like the ones that exasperate you in other people." Her voice softened and she met his gaze squarely. "And on Sundays you let emotion rule you completely. Whether you like it or not, you're one of us, Nick."

Nick stared at her in stunned silence. He should have felt that her knowledge of him was an invasion of his privacy, but he didn't. He felt a stirring excitement. It fluttered in his chest and grew strong, whipping through his mind, preceding an explosion of joy that knocked him right off his formerly-steadfast emotional feet.

This woman not only knew that he stood outside the warm cabin that was the world, she had somehow found a key to let him in. She wasn't merely telling him about the wonderful world she had found, she had magically discovered a way to share it with him.

Almost immediately he tried to back away. It couldn't be that simple—a few words and *zap!* the spell was gone. No, he thought distractedly. No, it wasn't the words. There was more. There was something magic in Jenny.

Stop it, he told himself firmly. He was being ridiculous. There was no magic—other than the natural magic of a beautiful, charming woman. Hundreds of other men had most likely found the same "magic," each one thinking himself unique for the time her attention was turned to him.

Nick recognized the logic of his explanation, but never had logical thinking been so unwelcome. He wanted the unexpected emotional transition to be real . . . and he wanted it to be something she had shared only with him.

The slapping sound of wind in the sails brought Nick's thoughts back to reality. Sitting up, he saw the sky had changed. Dark, green-edged clouds had come from nowhere, moving silently as they raced to capture the sun.

"Come on," he said, rising quickly to his feet to begin taking down the sails. "We need to make it back before this storm hits."

The heavens opened just a few yards from the dock. Fighting against the waves, it took Nick several attempts to maneuver the boat into the slip. As soon as it bumped into place, he turned to Jenny. "Run for the shelter beside the store!" he shouted to be heard above the wind and rain.

She shook her head stubbornly. "I'll stay and help."

Smiling with unbidden pleasure, Nick turned to his task. Together they fought the wind and the rain as they secured the boat.

She was a woman deserving of her name, he thought as they ran for a corrugated tin porch on the side of a store. Valiant.

They reached the shelter along with several other

people. Jenny laughed at him, her wet hair framing her face, sticking to her cheeks.

"I never saw anything come up so fast."

The woman who spoke had reached the porch just after Nick and Jenny. She was a little overweight and quite attractive, with once-red hair that had faded to a peachy brown. The man beside her bore a subtle resemblance to her. He was going bald and, unlike her, had a world-class nose, but the laugh lines around his eyes and mouth were the same as the woman's. Their gestures were also similar, as though they had lived together in harmony for a long time.

"I guess you're not from Texas," Jenny said. "We're famous for quick changes in weather. We don't get a chance to get bored with the weather."

The man chuckled. "I hope it doesn't snow. It would give Maureen an excuse to go shopping for sweaters."

"Bert," his wife said in laughing protest.

"The changes aren't quite that drastic," Jenny said, smiling at the affectionate teasing between the two.

The rain on the metal roof enclosed them in a solid wall of sound as they made polite small talk. Nick leaned against the wall and observed, just as he always did. For a moment he fought against resenting these people who'd forced him to be on the outside again, then he gave in to the feeling. Why shouldn't he resent them? He wanted time alone with Jenny, time to explore the way she made him feel.

After a while Bert began to pat his breast pocket. "How do matches know when to disappear? When

I'm in the car where I have a cigarette lighter, I have them coming out my ears, and at home I find matches breeding in drawers and spilling out of glass bowls everywhere. But the minute I get out somewhere like this, they vanish."

Jenny laughed. "I think there's some kind of law about that. The same one that says when you're late, you've got to put a thumb through your panty hose."

"Or when unexpected guests use your bathroom, you have to be out of toilet tissue," Maureen added.

"Or when you carefully pack for business trips, your socks have to disappear before you open the bag again," Nick said, grinning.

It was only when the others under the shelter began to add to the silly list that Nick realized what had happened. For just a moment he had felt close to these people. The shared laughter, the universal experiences, pulled him toward them. It should have been an ordinary incident, but to him it felt like something new and extraordinary.

As he met Jenny's eyes, he knew who was responsible. Once again she had pulled him into a feeling of brotherhood with the rest of humanity.

"You know," she said in a confiding whisper as she leaned closer, "there's something about the smell of people who have gotten unexpectedly wet. It always reminds me of childhood and my dog Petey."

He laughed, a sound filled with exuberance and pure delight. How had he lived so long without this? How had he managed to survive the dullness of a world without her?

Suddenly the laughter between them died, and they simply stood staring at each other. He had seen her beauty, but had he noticed before how soft her skin was, how totally desirable her lips? Turning so that his body shielded them from view, he bent to capture the magic in a kiss.

The touch of her lips was a revelation. So achingly sweet, so disturbingly beautiful. He was overwhelmed by an urgent need, a driving hunger. He couldn't have kept the kiss from deepening if the whole shelter had blown away. And amazingly, Jenny responded as though the kiss were as necessary to her as it was to him.

After a moment that reached for eternity, he pulled back, willing his pulse to stop racing, commanding his breathing to slow to normal. The trembling of response he felt in her didn't help calm him.

"Jenny," he said in a rough, almost harsh whisper, "why didn't I think of this when we were by ourselves in the middle of the lake?"

She shook her head, biting her lip as though she, too, had to fight desperately for control. He stroked her face gently and simply stared into her eyes, losing hold on all thought and reality as the minutes passed.

"Thank goodness that's over."

Maureen's voice brought them back. Nick moved away, putting some distance between their bodies as Jenny pushed her hair back from her face in a nervous gesture. During their seemingly intimate encounter, the shower had ended as quickly as it had begun.

"I guess I'd better get home." She glanced down at her clothes. "We're all wet, Nick."

He laughed as though she'd said something clever. But it wasn't what she said; it was simply the fact that she was Jenny and he had found her.

He walked her to the car in silence. But as she moved to slide into the driver's seat of a small yellow Chevrolet, he said, "Jenny?"

Turning her head slowly, she met his eyes. "Yes?"

He glanced away from her, then back again. "Give me a call on Monday . . . this time you'll get through."

For a moment her brow creased with confusion, then bright spots appeared on her cheeks. "The advertising," she said, shaking her head in bewilderment. "Oh, Lord, I forgot all about it."

She couldn't have said anything that would have pleased him more. The afternoon, the empathy between them, hadn't been about business. It hadn't been a sharp move on her part. She had forgotten as completely as he had why she had originally sought him out.

As he watched her drive away, he felt oddly deserted. Had she enchanted him? Was that why, for a little while, the world had seemed a different place? At that moment Nick came to a decision. He wouldn't question. He wouldn't poke and pry into his reactions. Jenny was like Sunday—she was emotion; she was sensation; she was pure feeling.

That Sunday had been the beginning. And ironically, it had been on a Sunday that the end had come. All the joy had been wiped out. And then Nick had cursed that day on the boat. If he had never met her, he would never have missed what she had brought to him.

Meeting her now, after all this time, he had wanted to grab her and shake her violently. *Why, Jenny?* he had wanted to shout. *Why did you leave me? Why did you stop loving me?*

But he couldn't think about it now, he told himself as he turned away from the window in Ralph Heywood's study. It was a stupid time to let memories take over. Nick was firmly planted in the present and had no use for the past, no use for the pain loving Jenny had brought.

"Never again, Jenny," he murmured, his jaw set as he walked to the door. "I won't ever let you do this to me again."

Four

Jenny walked into her apartment, slamming the door with enough force to make the windows rattle. Slumping into a chair, she threw one leg over the arm in an emphatic movement.

The apartment, with its bright chintz curtains and upwardly mobile furniture, wasn't home. It was a stopping place, as had been all her residences for the last two years. There was nothing uniquely Jenny in this room or the others. She didn't want to claim them as her own because she knew she was simply passing through on her way to an unidentifiable somewhere else.

For a long time she sat still, silently staring into space. It wasn't difficult finding the cause of the dizzying disorientation she felt. After being numb for two years, coming back to life was emotionally and physically punishing.

"Nick." The word was barely a whisper, but inside her head it was a scream that went on and on, a silent scream containing a thousand different passions.

What were he and the bride doing now? she wondered, shifting in discontent. Maybe they were on their way to the hotel. Maybe they were already at the hotel. Maybe Nick was undressing her, touching her.

Suddenly she picked up a throw pillow and hurled it forcefully across the room. "May you be overwhelmed by cellulite-dimpled thighs, Nicholas Reynolds!" she ground out through clenched teeth. "May you be smothered by triple-D breasts!"

Groaning, she curled up in a tight ball of misery, hating Nick . . . but especially hating the bride. Jenny never knew she could hate so deeply. Then, inevitably, as soon as she closed her eyes she felt guilt nagging at her. Her innate sense of fair play, dammit, wouldn't let her get away with insulting Elaine. Although she badly wanted to believe the bride was fat and dull and stupid, she knew none of those things were really true.

Was this how it was for all divorced women? she wondered dully. Would there always be hangover possessiveness? She knew that in the past two years there must have been a lot of women in Nick's life, but she hadn't had to meet any of them. It hadn't been difficult pretending they didn't exist, but pretense wasn't possible with the bride.

The bride. Nick's bride. Elaine was rich and beautiful and curvaceous, but it seemed strange to think she was really the kind of woman Nick wanted. Had Jenny misread him so completely? A year ago she would have said Elaine was the exact opposite of what Nick wanted. Even though the heiress had her good points, she was basically a clinger.

Jenny ran a shaky hand through her dark hair. It simply didn't make sense. If she was going to have any peace at all, she knew she would have to find the answer. Had she been mistaken about the reasons behind her failed marriage? Could it be that Nick had not stopped loving her because she had disappointed him? Maybe he had simply fallen out of love with her.

No, she thought as her heart beat against her chest with a painful thud, she couldn't accept that explanation. There was more to it, so much more. His eyes had held pain and accusation and disillusionment too often during those last months. She hadn't been mistaken. She had seen those eyes too often in her dreams, somber brown eyes that haunted her throughout the nightmare replays of the death of their marriage.

Maybe that was the answer, she thought dully. He went into his marriage with Jenny expecting her to be someone she wasn't and never could be. He had no such illusions about Elaine. Maybe Nick was protecting himself from the pain of disillusionment.

Sighing heavily, Jenny allowed the thought that the bride could be just exactly what Nick needed. There would be no turmoil in their relationship, none of the explosions that punctuated his first marriage.

No turmoil, an insidious voice whispered, but no fire either.

Jenny frowned. This was something that had nagged at her when she had seen Nick with the bride. At the time Jenny had been too emotionally strung out to examine it, but now it came back to worry her.

There had been no urgency in the bride's eyes when she looked at Nick. She hadn't caught her breath when he touched her. She hadn't sent silent messages that only he could interpret as a wish to be even closer to the heaven that was in his arms.

That's desire, Jenny told herself firmly. Not love. And desire without love was so lonely. Jenny had felt the loneliness too many times in the last months of her marriage to Nick. Physically he had never stopped needing her. But there had been no love on his side. He had shut her out emotionally. And it had left her devastatingly alone.

Jenny wiped the dampness from her cheeks. Desire without love was empty, she thought.

All animosity for the couple drained away, leaving her curiously bereft. Maybe this is objectivity, Jenny realized with a caustic smile. Nick had always preached objectivity; maybe she had finally learned how to reach that state.

"Simply put yourself on a torture rack for a couple of years and *voilà!*—objectivity," she murmured to the empty room. "Once you discover emotions can be killers, you positively embrace the unemotional perspective."

But Jenny couldn't wipe out all feeling. Never once in the two years they had been apart had she tried to convince herself she didn't care for Nick. She knew, however, that they were bad for each other. Right from the beginning they had been all wrong.

She wanted more for Nick this time. He deserved to get all he wanted from life. Although she secretly doubted it, Jenny prayed that Elaine was the answer. *Please let him be happy this time*, she begged silently.

Exasperated with her moodiness, Jenny rose abruptly to her feet and walked into the bedroom. Nick's happiness shouldn't be so important to her, she told herself as she began to strip off her clothes. He was no longer her concern. Technically they might still be married, but emotionally they were well and truly divorced. It was none of her business how Nick and the bride felt about each other.

Stepping into the shower, Jenny let the cool water flow over her face, trying to ease the emotional storm seeing Nick had caused.

Could it be that she was still feeling guilty about the way she had let Nick down in their marriage? she wondered as she idly soaped her body. Although she refused to think about those last hellish months, she had never tried to deny to herself that she had been a terrible wife to Nick.

But then, she had always known she would be, even way back at the beginning. When they had first started seeing each other, it hadn't seemed important that she wasn't the right kind of wife for him. Their very differences had attracted them to each other and intrigued them both.

It was only after they had made love for the first time that Jenny knew for certain they were headed for trouble.

Stepping from the shower, her blue eyes were unfocused as she dried off. She couldn't think about the first time. Even now, so many years later, the memory of that night had the power to make her weak. There had been a beauty, rare and magnificent, in their coming together, a beauty that had stunned her. Jenny hadn't expected anything more than physical pleasure. But the truth and honesty in the feelings they had created together went beyond the physical. It had been so overwhelming, Jenny had felt a fear deeper than any she had ever known. Why should such beauty come to her? Something of this magnitude didn't happen to ordinary people.

After the first night their relationship had changed irrevocably. Most of the time, at least on the surface, they were like best friends or brother and sister, teasing and laughing, talking until all hours of the night, dealing with trivialities with as much enthusiasm as they dealt with the meaningful issues of life. And then, when she least expected it, a look or a touch would pass between them and the passion that always lay beneath the surface would flare up and rage out of control.

Jenny had been so enthralled, so mesmerized by the wonder of it all that she hadn't allowed herself to speculate about the future. When a magnificent gift is given, it may also be taken away, and that was something she couldn't face.

She had been completely under the control of her dazzled emotions when she had accepted his proposal of marriage. Reason had played no part in her acceptance. It had taken weeks for reality to catch up with her. But when it finally hit, it hit hard.

Like a revelation from a thundering god, it had suddenly struck her that time was moving too fast, that in a few short weeks she would be married to a man who didn't really know her, a man she didn't really know.

Three weeks after promising to marry Nick, she had sat staring at the walls, feeling pressure grow inside her chest as she waited for him to arrive.

Over and over again she told herself it was all wrong. He considered every move; she dove in headfirst. His life was organized down to the last detail; she liked to let life surprise her. He was intense; she was loose. He was steering a strict course through life; she was simply along for the ride, enjoying the scenery as she went.

The damning list went on and on until Jenny finally decided it was time for her to face facts. Against all reason Nick thought she was wonderful—at least for this moment he did. How long before he began to feel only irritation for her illogical approach to life? How long before he began to share his mother's disenchanted view of her?

She should never have promised to marry him, she thought with mounting desperation. She had become enthralled by a fairy tale, believing for a while that it was real. And when arrangements had been made for the wedding, when they were involved in plans for the future, she finally saw that she couldn't go through with it. She had to break it off before it went any further.

By the time Nick arrived, Jenny had worked herself into a state of panic. She had forgotten to get dressed for their date and still wore the sweatshirt she had inherited from a long-forgotten college boyfriend. Her hair was a mess from the many times she had run her fingers through it and her makeup nonexistent.

Walking into the apartment, he immediately pulled her into his arms, kissing her with a passion that drove her resolutions from her mind.

But when he leaned back to observe her with a frown, all her fears came back.

"Yes, I know," she said grimly. "I look like something out of *Night of the Living Dead*." She pulled out of his arms. "This is the real me. I look like this"—she studied his reaction—"a lot."

He chuckled. "You sound like you're in the middle of a blue funk. It's not the time of the month for you to throw things at me."

She bit her lip. He sounded so happy as he tried to provoke her with a statement that would ordinarily have started a verbal war. How was she going to get through this? "Nick—"

"Something's really wrong, isn't it?" He was instantly sympathetic, his eyes concerned. "Is it your job? Do you want to sit down and talk about it?"

She shook her head with unnecessary vehemence. "It's not the job. Nick—oh, God!" She turned away in frustration. "I can't do it, Nick."

"Do what?"

His words were casual, but Jenny sensed an instant wariness. It was crazy to drag it out. She had to be strong enough to do what was right. Knowing any strength she possessed would disappear the first time she looked into his eyes, she kept her back to him.

"I can't marry you." The words were a faint whisper, barely audible to her own ears.

"I—I don't think I heard you."

"I can't marry you," she said, this time making the words separate and emphatic. "It won't work."

For a long time there was only silence in the room, dragging out until she was weak with tension. Then he gave a short, hoarse laugh. "Sometimes I can't keep up with your sense of humor."

When he paused, she could feel him waiting for her response, but there was nothing she could say.

"I don't find this joke particularly funny, Jenny," he said, his voice containing anger and some other element she couldn't identify.

She swung around, her eyes pleading for his understanding. "It won't work, Nick. It just won't work. Let me back out without making a big deal out of it."

"Big deal?" He moved away from her, staring at her as though he had never seen her before. "Don't make a big deal out of it?" His brown eyes caught fire. "You cut my throat and watch me bleed, then tell me not to make a big deal out of it. This doesn't make any sense. We were making plans last night—this morning at breakfast, for heaven's sake. What happened?"

She pushed the hair off her forehead, glancing away from the fury in his harsh face. "Nothing happened—oh, hell, I just decided it was all wrong."

He grabbed her shoulders, forcing her to look at him, forcing her to witness the frantic fear that had taken the place of anger in his dark eyes. "Don't tell me nothing," he ground out. "I want to know why you suddenly decided you can't marry me. What did I do wrong?" He shook her hard. "Come on, Jenny, give me reasons. Do I talk too much . . . laugh too loud? What is it?"

Jenny could see him striving for control and it tore at her heart. With a trembling hand he touched her face. "Listen, darling, listen . . . this can't happen. We can't let it happen. You love me—I know you do. Maybe not as much as I love you, but, dammit, *you love me*." His lips were white as he forced the words out. All Jenny could do was shake her head incoherently. "Whatever the problem is, just tell me. We can work it out." He clasped both her hands to his chest, his dark eyes pleading. "Just tell me, Jenny."

She couldn't answer him. She could only stare with wide open, pain-filled eyes as an overwhelming pressure grew inside her. Suddenly his expression changed; it went totally blank. Dropping her hands, he turned away from her.

"I guess I'm being pretty dense," he said with an odd quirk in his voice. "All this time I've been fooling myself, haven't I? You don't love me at all. That's what's behind this, isn't it?"

She felt isolated and more lonely than she would have ever believed possible. He sounded cool and calm, but Jenny knew him too well now. Nick wasn't cool; he was hurting, and his pain was suddenly too much for her to bear.

"No!" The word was almost a groan. Moving quickly, she wrapped her arms around him, burying her face in his broad chest. "Don't ever say that," she whispered harshly, her hands clenching and unclenching in his jacket. "Don't ever say that again. I'm sorry; oh, God, I'm so sorry. I just got scared. But it's gone now." She reached up to touch his face, her movements frantic as she tried to smooth away the damage she had done. "I promise it's gone."

For a long time they simply held each other. As Nick began to relax the tight control he had on his emotions, deep tremors shook his body. It was then that Jenny made a resolution. If he needed her this much, then she would make it all right, she vowed silently. Maybe she wasn't the right person for him now, but she would fake it until she could be.

As though he had heard her silent promise, Nick pulled back a little, framing her face with his hands. "Just love me, Jenny," he said in a rough whisper. "That's all I need. If you love me, we can work anything out."

"No matter what happens, I'll never stop loving you, Nick," she whispered, looking up at him. "I couldn't. Loving you is as much a part of me as my brain, my heart. Trying not to love you would be like trying not to think or feel. It's simply not possible."

"It had better not be." The words were a less than gentle threat. "That first night you promised me forever. I won't . . . I can't settle for anything less."

She shook her head vehemently. "Only forever for us, Nick. Only forever."

Suddenly he gripped her shoulders and shook her so hard her teeth rattled. "Then what in hell was all this about?" he shouted furiously.

She laughed in relief that the emotional storm was past. "It was last-minute nerves. Haven't you ever heard of bridal jitters? I've never been married before. What if I screw it up?"

He exhaled slowly, resting his forehead on hers. "I've never been married before either. I'm just as likely to screw it up as you are. If that happens, we'll handle it. We can tackle anything as long as we're together." He slapped her sharply on the derriere. "Lord, you know how to keep things exciting, don't you? I'll let you get away with it this time, but never again—understand?" When she nodded, he began walking her toward the bedroom. "Okay, I've had enough of this. I'm ready for forever to start." He looked down at her, his brown eyes flaring with growing excitement. "Let's do it tonight, Jenny. Let's not wait."

She stared at him in confusion, then in astonishment. "You mean get married? But our friends . . . your mother . . . all the plans we've made."

"To hell with the plans," he said carelessly. "I want you tied to me tonight. We've waited too long already. I should have carried you off the day you stowed away on the *Reunion.* We'll take Harry and Sharon with us, and my mother can give us a huge reception later."

Jenny hadn't been able to resist his enthusiasm. But then, she had never been able to resist Nick in anything for very long. They had married that same night in a wild, impromptu ceremony that had included not only Harry and Sharon, but several of the justice of the peace's relatives, who just happened to be visiting.

It had seemed at the time like a wonderful beginning. But even back then it had not been perfect. Mrs. Reynolds had been mortally offended. There had been no reception. And it hadn't lasted forever. It hadn't even lasted four years. Three years, two months, and four days. Then no more Nick and Jenny.

After such a wild beginning an explosive ending might have been forecast. But the end of their relationship had been just as unpredictable as the rest. The grand finale hadn't come with a bang but with a whimper.

Glancing up, Jenny saw sunlight pouring through the curtains. She had been up all night. She wasn't normally the kind of person to wallow in painful memories, but this time it had helped. Without realizing it, she had reached a decision. She owed Nick. She had made promises she had been unable to keep. At least she could give him a clean beginning to his future.

She glanced at the clock, then went to the phone. Harry picked it up on the third ring.

"Harry," she said, "it's me, Jenny."

"Good morning, beautiful Jenny. Sharon's in the shower. She can call you back in fifteen minutes."

"Actually, it's you I need to talk to."

"Good. You wanna flirt?" he teased. "What Sharon doesn't know won't hurt her. Wait—don't tell me you're calling to cancel dinner on Wednesday night."

"Wednesday?" she asked in confusion, then sighed heavily. "I forgot all about it. As a matter of fact, I will have to cancel, but that's not why I called."

He must have heard something in her voice. "What's up? You sound strange."

"Not as strange as I feel," she said, her voice wry. Inhaling, she plunged ahead. "Harry, can you arrange a Mexican divorce?"

"A divorce? For who?"

She swallowed heavily. "For me."

There was a long silence. "Did you do something stupid out there in California?"

She gave a broken laugh. "No, I did something stupid here in Fort Worth. Did you hear about that Mexican divorce scam? A lawyer named Jesus Escobar?"

Harry was quick. "Oh, hell," he breathed warily. "Your divorce to Nick?"

"You got it."

Harry burst out laughing. His enjoyment was frank and lasting.

"Does—" he began, gulping back his laughter. "Does Nick know about this?"

"I told him yesterday . . . at his reception."

That set him off again. Resignedly, Jenny allowed him to continue for several minutes, then muttered grimly, "You're very peculiar, Harry."

"I'm sorry," he said, still chuckling, "but Nick, the poor sap, didn't even know you were back in town. I tried to tell him, but he refused to listen. Oh, my, oh, my, oh, my—so I missed all the fireworks. The aunt with the mustache probably had me cornered." He laughed again. "It's perfect. Like fate or something." When she remained silent, he cleared his throat noisily. "I know this doesn't seem funny to you, but wow, I would have given a nickel to see Nick's face." He laughed again. "Lord, I love it."

"I'm always glad to provide wholesome entertainment for my friends," she said dryly. "But do you think you could stop giggling long enough to help me out here?"

"Right—yes, of course," he said, struggling to keep his voice serious. "Give me half an hour and I'll see what I can set up."

As soon as she replaced the receiver, Jenny headed for the bedroom. It didn't take long to pack enough for a quick trip to Mexico. It was what came next that took time. She would have to let Nick know what she was doing. There was so much she could say, but eventually she realized it had all been said.

Nick, she wrote, *I got us into this and I'll get us*

out. Since Harry is handling the arrangements, you can be sure that this time it will take. I'll get in touch with you through Harry as soon as it's final. Jenny.

As soon as it's final. Jenny didn't want to think about why the words brought a tightness to her chest. It was time for her to get on with her life. It was time to let go. Maybe this time it really would be final.

Nick pushed aside his half-eaten breakfast, surreptitiously studying the woman seated across from him. The raised white-draped bed behind her was a perfect background for the white lace negligee she wore. Even at this hour of the morning her makeup was perfect, applied with a skilled hand to make her look dewy fresh.

"Why are you frowning?" Elaine asked gently.

Nick shook his head. "I'm sorry, Elaine. I'm sorry your wedding day, and now your honeymoon, was ruined. I wanted it to be just right for you." He grimaced. "Not a very good introduction to married life, I'm afraid."

"Don't be silly," she said, reaching out to squeeze his hand. "It was also your wedding and your honeymoon. It's an inconvenience for us both, but that's all." She smiled. "I don't expect perfection out of life. You know that." She paused, biting her lip. "I—I hope your room was comfortable. I'm sorry we couldn't be together. You do understand how I feel about . . . about everything?"

He moved his lips in a wry, inwardly turned smile. "There's no need for you to apologize. We didn't agree to have an affair; we agreed to have a marriage."

Nick tried to keep his tone light. He would never be able to tell her how relieved he had been that she hadn't wanted to share a bedroom the night before. It was too soon after seeing Jenny, and his emotions were too raw.

"Nicky?"

Elaine's soft voice brought his thoughts back to her. She avoided his gaze as she carefully refolded her napkin. "Does Jenny know why we married?"

Although she tried to make the question sound casual, Nick sensed her embarrassment. "Of course not," he said, his voice sharper and more abrupt than he had intended. "It's none of her business."

She sighed in relief. "I know it's silly of me, but I'd rather no one knew, especially Jenny."

"Why especially Jenny?"

She shook her head helplessly. "It's a woman thing. Women tend to judge other women harshly."

He frowned. "Jenny's not the kind to judge anyone."

"I'm sure she's not," she said quickly. "Oh, I told you it was silly. It's just that she seemed like such a strong person, so sure of herself. I would rather she didn't know that I'm not normal, that I'm inadequate . . . emotionally."

"Elaine, darling," he said, feeling uncomfortable with her openness. "You're being too hard on yourself. Our marriage may be based on reason rather than emotion, but that doesn't make it wrong." He shrugged. "In fact, what we've planned is just exactly right for us. And it concerns only us. So no one else's opinion matters."

"Yes, you're right. I know you are. But I still would rather she didn't know."

"You don't have to worry," he said, the lines in his face growing harsher. "I can't see myself discussing our relationship with my ex-wife."

Or anything else for that matter, he thought grimly. He would get Harry to handle the divorce, and there would be no need for him to talk to Jenny again. Just the thought of her made him angry. He had finally gotten it all together, had finally pulled his life together and found a direction for the future, only to have her pop up and destroy everything. Maybe Jenny would always be a nagging ache in his heart, but he refused to let that stop him from living.

A knock on the door brought his thoughts abruptly back to the present. When he opened the door, a black-uniformed bellboy handed him an envelope. After tipping the boy, Nick closed the door, opened the envelope, and pulled the note out. He glanced at it quickly, then began to swear softly, violently.

"What is it?" Elaine asked anxiously, examining his features. "Is it bad news?"

"*Damn her.* Damn her to hell." He raked a hand through his hair. "I'm sorry, Elaine, but—just give me a minute. I've got to call Harry."

Five minutes later, when he hung up the phone, he looked grimmer than ever. Although Harry had answered all his questions seriously, Nick had heard the laughter in his voice. Sadistic bastard.

Glancing up, he found Elaine standing and watching in silence. He shook his head. "It's Jenny. She's decided to take things into her own hands and get another divorce."

"But—but that's good, isn't it?"

"You don't know Jenny. She's a disaster waiting for a chance to happen." His strong features grew harsh. "Not this time," he muttered. "Because, by all that's holy, I'll be there to make sure she gets it right."

Inhaling deeply, he forced himself to relax. "Elaine, I'm more sorry than I can tell you, darling, but I think you'd better go on to France without me. As soon as I get all this straightened out, I'll join you." He put his arm around her shoulders and smiled down at her, pretending he was calm, pretending he wasn't thinking about how it would feel to throttle his almost, but not quite, ex-wife. "We can redo our vows there in peace, then get on with our lives."

"But Nicky," she said hesitantly. "Where are you going?"

He smiled, and there was no pretense. It was a smile that held vengeance. "I'm going to a place called San Lazaro Ruiz to make damn sure Jenny doesn't mess it up again."

Five

San Lazaro Ruiz, Veracruz, Mexico

In 1435 a small group of Aztec Indians gathered together their wives, children, and meager possessions and left the thriving capital city of Tenochtitlán. They were outcasts, the black sheep of a majestic, fearless society. Heading east, they began a last-ditch effort at survival. Individually and as a group, they had tried and failed at everything they turned their hands to—crafts, farming, and fishing. The poor souls weren't even decent sacrifice material.

To the east lay the wide water. Surely, they reasoned, one or the other of the gods would look with favor upon them. If they named their new settlement after a god, perhaps their luck would change.

In the first four years they changed the name of their village fifteen times, but other than one spring, when a large fish jumped into one of the Indians' boats, the gods, for the most part, looked the other way. Because of the fish, they kept the name Xipe Totec, after the god of springtime and regrowth, for seventh-three years.

In time the villagers grew used to being poor and inept. Their badly built houses collapsed with the first sign of strong winds; their crops shriveled in the sun; their animals refused to breed, and fish eluded their nets. It became something of a tradition, passed down from generation to incompetent generation.

In the summer of 1543, the year of the great pig war, the village's name was changed for the last two times. Keeping with tradition, the present-generation villagers were inefficient warriors; they tended to run and hide at the least hint of trouble. The closest they came to courage was to call enemies insulting names behind their backs.

But in that summer a challenge was presented to them that couldn't possibly be ignored. A village several miles to the north had sent warriors into Xipe Totec to steal the sacred mascot—a huge, pampered pig that wandered through the village at will—intending the animal for a barbecue party the chief was to throw for his friends and business associates.

The young men of Xipe Totec, reluctantly recognizing that the insult could not be overlooked, changed the name of their village to Huitzilopochtli for the god of war, fortified themselves with fermented cactus juice, grabbed their *atlatls*, and went to war.

Women, children, and old men cheered them as the warriors marched by on their way north. This courage business wasn't so bad, the men decided as they nodded in noble condescension on their way out of the village.

Several hours and five miles later, after the hot sun had sweated the *octli* out of them, they began to recall rumors they had heard about the village to the north. Someone had heard that the men there were giants with prominent foreheads and hairy hands, who were trained to rob a man of his masculinity in a particularly painful way.

This, decided the warriors, was something that needed careful thought. Finding shade under a rocky overhang, they sat to discuss the problem. If they turned back, the old men and children would spit on them with contempt. And worse, the women would refuse to sleep with them. On the other hand, if they went forward and attacked the village, they would be dead or, at the very least, emasculated. Honor and glory would be wasted on dead men. And what good was a woman's adulation to a man who had no manhood.

At that moment the ugliest, scrawniest iguana that ever walked the vast Aztec empire staggered out of the underbrush. Most of the harassed warriors paid no attention, but one young man watched. Close behind the iguana came a strange-looking man. It was Father Juanito, a Spanish priest originally bound for the capital city, who had become lost from his guide and stumbled onto the warriors by mere chance after several exhausting days in the wilderness.

As was their custom, the warriors trembled in fear before the mild-mannered stranger. But the young man who had been watching, seeing that the priest meant them no harm, suddenly had a brainstorm.

What if, he asked his friends, this were a messenger from the gods—didn't he look the part, with his strange coloring and clothing and indecipherable language. Perhaps this messenger brought the iguana from the gods as a replacement for the pig? If ever an animal resembled their village and their people, it was this pathetic-looking creature. Surely this was a sign that they were to go back to the village with this lizard as their new mascot, and the messenger as proof of their claims. Why, he told them with growing excitement, it was almost as if the god of war himself had appeared before them and given them orders. They couldn't disobey a god, could they? The women and children would stand in awe of warriors who had actually been singled out by a god.

The young man's idea was accepted unanimously and with great relief. Furthermore, by the time the motley crew returned to the safety of their village, each was convinced he had actually been blessed by an Aztec god, and legend recorded their version of the story.

After spending many months trying to leave, Father Juanito finally became resigned to the fact that God had brought him to this ill-favored village. Girding his loin, he changed the village's name to San Lazaro Ruiz and began to convert the natives to Christianity.

The village's name remained, as did the Christianity and the hereditary ineptitude of the villagers. That is, until 1952. In that year San Lazaro Ruiz found its true calling. At last the people were experts at something. And, praise be to God, it was something they thoroughly enjoyed—catering to wealthy Americans who wanted to dissolve their marriages in the fastest way possible. In 1952, San Lazaro Ruiz discovered the quickie divorce.

Now, as Jenny walked along Xipe Totec Boulevard, the main street of the village and northern boundary of Huitzilopochtli Square, she had no knowledge of the village's history. She knew only that this was where Harry had sent her for the divorce.

"Señorita, señorita! You wish to buy a momento of San Lazaro Ruiz? I sell only the best merchandise." The teenaged boy waved a dark hand toward the brightly colored stuffed animals on the sidewalk behind him. "I have just such a thing for a beautiful lady."

Jenny shook her head in smiling regret. "I'm afraid I have one already. Thanks anyway."

All day she had tried to consider it a vacation. She wore the floppy straw hat that identified her as a tourist, and her purchases, including an enormous lavender paper flower, overflowed from the woven shoulder bag she carried awkwardly under one arm. She had taken snapshots of the picturesque but poorly built church and had even tasted the wares of several street vendors.

It hadn't helped. She knew very well it wasn't a vacation. This was Jenny's second visit to Mexico, and her present trip was no less depressing than the first. No one should have to sit through a rerun of her own divorce, she thought as he walked toward the Bay of Campeche.

That's probably what hell will be like, she realized with irrepressible humor, some poor damned schmuck, forced to go through an eternity of divorces.

The magnificent colors of the Mexican sunset

barely penetrated her consciousness as she headed slowly for her bungalow. The small, elegant cottage Harry had reserved for her was part of the Moreno Hotel, a large modern structure overlooking the brilliant blue water of the bay. Harry must have known how she would hate being in the main part of the hotel with all the other waiting women, some who moved about in frantic jubilance, others openly grieving.

Palm trees and huge flowering bushes along the beach made an exciting, exotic background that by rights should have been seen by someone more eager to appreciate its beauty.

After fumbling in her shoulder bag for the key to the bungalow, she had to maneuver around the ridiculous paper flower to unlock the door. Upon entering, she stood just inside the room for a second as she allowed her eyes to adjust to the shadows.

"It's about time."

Jenny inhaled in a sharp gasp. Across the room Nick stood leaning against the wall by the window. The pale blue knit sport shirt and khaki slacks he wore with such casual elegance made him look at first glance like a thousand other American tourists. There was certainly nothing in his appearance that should cause Jenny's heart to leap in her chest. Nothing except the fact that he was Nick, in Mexico, near enough for her to touch.

Weariness disappeared instantly as she felt exhilaration flood her limbs. It was like coming out of hibernation after a long, cold winter. Suddenly Jenny felt vibrant, alive—and gloriously, furiously angry. What in the name of heaven was he doing here?

Dropping her packages on the couch, she fought to control her features as she slowly turned to face him. "This is just what I needed to cap off a truly memorable day," she said slowly. "What happened? Did your plane make a wrong turn on its way to the Riviera?"

His eyes narrowed at her flippant greeting, and he rubbed one palm with the knuckles of his other hand in a gesture familiar to her. "I'm not going to give you a chance to screw it up again," he said slowly. "I'll be right here to make sure it's all legal this time."

She ran her gaze over him slowly, raising one questioning brow. "What do you think you can do that I can't? I'm perfectly capable of cutting the strings on my own." She met his eyes squarely, stubbornly. "I can handle it, Nick."

Frustration and exasperation caused him to take an involuntary step toward her. "Is that right? Try again, Jenny. This is me, remember? The man who lived with you for over three years. I've got names and dates and places to prove you've never handled anything without bringing disaster to both of us. I remember the dinner parties without a hostess until dessert was served because something diverted your attention and you simply forgot we were having guests. I remember having to fight insurance investigators over my gutted shell of an office because you decided cherries jubilee on my desk would be romantic. I remember my mother's surprise birthday party that I—may the dear Lord forgive my naivete—asked you to arrange. The birthday party that turned into all-out war because you decided to invite the woman my mother hates most in the entire world. I—"

"Wrong," Jenny said, smiling sweetly. "I believe I can claim that honor."

Nick was on a roll and wasn't about to let her interruption stop him. "I remember the quiet weekend I had planned so carefully, the weekend I had been looking forward to after months of nonstop work, I remember that same weekend being trampled beneath the feet of the entire population of Fort Worth's Vietnamese orphanage."

Moving forward, he grasped her arm between hard fingers. "I remember," he said between clenched teeth, "that I was supposed to be divorced *two years ago*!"

Pulling away from him, she brushed the hair from her forehead and gave him an airy look. "So what's your point?"

When his eyes blazed she sighed. "Okay, okay. So I've made a few mistakes. But Harry set this up for me. Surely you trust Harry?"

"I don't trust anyone where you're concerned," he said, his voice harassed and emphatic. "You could disarrange the plans of the KGB. I'm here, Jenny. And I'll stay until we are well and truly divorced."

She stared at him for a moment, then shook her head. "Really, Nick. You're going to have to do something about your paranoia." The expression on his face had her backing away warily. "What the heck," she said generously. "You want to stay— stay." Frowning, she glanced at the door. "How did you get in here anyway? I know they're loose down here, but don't tell me they hand out keys to their guests' rooms to any Tom, Dick, or Harry that comes along."

He laughed shortly. "They're definitely not loose concerning their guests. They wouldn't tell me where you were until I had produced identification proving that I'm your beloved husband."

She studied him with quickened interest. Nick must have been desperate to have claimed that relationship. "So where did you stash the bride? I'm sure she's eager for your company and, of course, I don't want to keep you, so—"

"Elaine's on her way to Europe," he said, smiling with wicked pleasure at having thwarted her obvious attempt to get rid of him. "I'll catch up with her when the divorce is final."

Jenny turned away, unwilling to have him read her expression. She had been thinking about the divorce all day. She had come to the conclusion that people witless enough to marry in the first place deserved what they got.

"Well, she shouldn't have long to wait," she said with forced brightness. "I have an appointment with the lawyer at eleven tomorrow. A man named Matteo Nuñez." She glanced over her shoulder. "Where are you staying?"

"Here."

"You mean at the Moreno?"

"I mean here—in this room." Jenny definitely didn't like the smile curving his strong lips. "Someone at the hotel overbooked. The place is overflowing with soon-to-be-free women and insurance salesmen from Nebraska. Since this is the only decent hotel in town, we'll have to share."

Her heart started pounding as she backed away from him again. "Oh, no, Nick," she said, shaking her head emphatically. "Not here. Pitch a tent, rent a Winnebago, weave a hut—anything. But you're not staying here."

He laughed in genuine amusement. "What's the matter, afraid I'll strangle you in the middle of the night?" His gaze slid over her body. "Or isn't it your neck you're worried about? Don't get your hopes up, Jenny. The couch folds out. I'm sure I'll be very comfortable. If we try real hard, we can probably avoid killing each other for a couple of days."

"Don't make a bet on that," she muttered, running a hand through her hair. "Won't this seem a little strange to the bride? Or will you just keep quiet about it? You're real good at keeping things to yourself, aren't you, Nick?"

As though she were inside his head, she felt the physical effort he made to stay calm. After a long, tense moment he produced a tight smile. "Whether you like it or not, we're going to be seeing a lot of each other in the next few days. I think it would be better if we kept personalities out of this."

"Oh, by all means let's keep personalities out of our divorce," she said, her eyes sparkling with laughter. "Maybe we should think of it as a corporate split."

"Jenny." The softly spoken word was an unconcealed threat.

"Remember—no strangling," she reminded him cheekily, stretching her back to work out a kink. "My feet are killing me, and I think some Mexican bugs are seeking political asylum in my hair."

He stared at her for a moment, then said softly, "Spanish flies?"

A surprised laugh caught in her throat. She

would never get used to his black humor. "Something like that," she murmured, watching as he moved her shoulder bag to sit on the couch.

"What in hell is this?" he asked, pulling a neon-pink stuffed animal from the bag.

She pushed her hair back on her forehead. "I think it's supposed to be an iguana. For some reason they're hanging all over the village. Maybe they ward off bad spirits or something." At his skeptical look she shrugged. "Yes, it's weird; the whole village is weird. Their souvenirs fall apart, the buildings look like they were built in the dark, and the food is terrible. But don't blame me. Harry chose this place; he's your friend and lawyer."

"He may be my friend and lawyer, but I've never said the man wasn't strange."

She laughed at his dry tone, feeling a little of the tension drain away as she left the room for her bath. Ten minutes later, her hair curling damply around her face, she wondered what she should wear but finally shrugged in unconcern. What the hell, she thought, there's no one here to impress. Nick knew her too well. He knew that being comfortable for her meant no restrictions —no stockings, no shoes, no makeup, and no bra.

She pulled out of the closet a blue silk jersey caftan that had seen better days. The hem drooped inelegantly on one side, and snags gave it a rough texture it hadn't originally had. She brushed back her wet hair, leaving her face bare of makeup.

In the living room Nick stood beside a table set for two. A hotel cart loaded with covered trays was sitting next to the table.

"I ordered it before you got back," he said, indicating the food. "I hope—my Lord, do you still have that thing?" he said, staring at the caftan. "It should have been in the rag bag years ago."

She shrugged. "I like it." The smell of food reached her, causing her stomach to roll in queasy reaction. "I think I'll skip dinner—too much junk food today." Sitting at the table, she picked up the wine bottle. "I'll have a glass of wine and watch you eat." After pouring a glass of wine, she said politely, "How is your mother?"

He raised one brow. "Chitchat, Jenny?" When she shifted uneasily, he said, "She's fine, as always."

Jenny nodded, staring at the glass in her hand. "I bet she's tickled pink about your marriage to Elaine."

He was silent long enough to make her uncomfortable, then he said, "I think we'd better avoid talking about my marriage to Elaine."

"Okay by me," she said. "I just thought I'd give you a chance to rave about her virtues."

"Why did you leave California?"

She raised her gaze to his, immediately feeling the impact of his dark eyes. "The work was fantastic, the weather was glorious, the people were a joy. I tried to find fault with it, but I couldn't. The truth is I missed Texas. California wasn't even a close substitute. I didn't fit in because I didn't want to fit in. When I figured that out, I knew it was time to come home."

He nodded absentmindedly. "What happened to the game show host you were dating?"

"Kurt?" She laughed. "How on earth did you hear about him?"

He stared at a spot just beyond her shoulders,

not quite meeting her eyes. "I suppose Harry must have mentioned you were seeing him."

Jenny leaned forward, her eyes sparkling. "I wish you could have met him. His hair didn't move. I swear, Nick. A hurricane wouldn't have ruffled it. It was getting thin in the back, so he sort of swirled it around." She grinned in reminiscence. "He spent a lot of time talking about the contribution of game shows to American culture. But of course," she said, mimicking Kurt's carefully controlled tones, "people don't know a wonderful thing when they see it. According to Kurt, murder, robbery, and deviant sex would sweep the United States if game shows ever went off the air.

"And speaking of television," she said, studying his seemingly relaxed features, "whoever is doing your California commercials stinks. They're missing the target audience completely."

Nick nodded. "Yes, I know. Their contract is up. I'm giving the work back to Fowler's."

"Good," she said in satisfaction. "Maybe I'll get the account."

He frowned. "You're back with Fowler's?"

"For over a month now," she confirmed. "Old man Fowler lectured me like crazy about gypsies who flit from one job to another, but he took me back."

"He'd be a fool not to," Nick said quietly. "You're the best they've ever had."

She was surprised and touched by his confidence in her. "Why, thank you, Nick," she said, her voice warm as she met his dark eyes.

He stiffened, and there was no answering warmth in his gaze. "There's nothing to thank me for.

Facts are facts. Just because you're a calamity on a personal level doesn't mean you're not a top-notch professional."

Jenny sucked in a sharp breath at the cut. He might as well have slapped her face. Clenching her fists, she leaned forward, meeting his gaze squarely. "And just because you're a cold fish—personally speaking, that is," she added with a deceptively pleasant smile, "doesn't mean you don't know excellence when you see it."

For several explosive seconds they merely glared at each other, then suddenly Jenny burst out laughing. Nick stared at her for a moment, then grinned reluctantly.

"We should have expected this," she said, leaning back in the chair as she relaxed completely for the first time since she had found him in her room. "I don't think either of us can take this sophisticated, civil stuff for too long."

He shook his head ruefully. "The whole thing has thrown me for a loop. 'Just when you thought it was safe to go back into the water.' I don't think my brain has caught up yet with what's happening."

"I know what you mean," she murmured. Inhaling, she pushed back the chair and stood, giving him a slight smile. "I think—discretion being the better part of valor—that during this lull in hostilities I'll say good night."

"Discretion, my ass," he said, grinning broadly. "You're a coward."

She curtsied, blandly accepting the label as she walked away. At the door to the bedroom she paused, keeping her gaze carefully away from his. "Nick," she said hesitantly, "I really am sorry for this mess. You must hate me for all the trouble I've brought you."

She stood for a while listening to the silence, then, feeling dreadfully weary, opened the door. As she began to close the door behind her, she finally heard his voice.

"I could never hate you, Jenny," Nick said, his voice clear and curiously devoid of emotion. "I've tried, but I can't."

Fighting tears, Jenny stood for a moment, then nodded her head in understanding and closed the door.

Nick stared at the door, feeling as if every nerve were stretched to the breaking point. He knew there would be no sleep for him tonight. The room was too full of memories. His head was too full of Jenny, damn her.

After pushing the cart with their barely-touched dinner outside the front door, he used the other door to the bathroom and took a cool shower. Fifteen minutes later he reentered the small sitting room. His hair was damp and he wore the bottom half of a pair of silk pajamas Elaine had given him the previous Christmas. It was as much of a concession to convention as he cared to make.

The couch converted easily into a bed but creaked protestingly when he stretched out on it. Lying in the dark, he fought to relax, but it was a losing battle. He was much too keyed up to sleep.

It wasn't only the situation that bothered him. Now that he had time to think about it, there was something about Jenny that he had missed at the reception. She was still vital and quick-witted, but it seemed to him the brightness had a sharper edge. There was an underlying element he had not seen before. Wariness? Bitterness? he wondered with a frown. Was he responsible for it, or had something happened to her in California?

On the surface she seemed the same vibrant Jenny. She still wore the same rag of a caftan. She had always hung on to things well past their usefulness. Nick had assumed it had something to do with her childhood. Orphaned at the age of six, she had been raised by an aunt and uncle, who had several children of their own. He had met the large, boisterous family only once, but he could see that it had probably been next to impossible for Jenny to have things that were exclusively hers. Although she never spoke about it, he had decided early on that it was for this reason she hoarded things in boxes and on shelves, obscure treasures that meant nothing to anyone but her.

He wondered if she still slept in his shirt. The last time he had seen it, three of the buttons were missing, but she always refused to throw it out because it was comfortable. She had never known how provocative the damn thing was. But then, Jenny would look sexy in a burlap bag.

As he thought of her in the next room, sprawled out on the bed, her long legs showing beneath the loose cotton shirt, Nick shifted his position restlessly. He couldn't let himself think of her. If he remembered the way she looked, he would remember the way she felt and the way she tasted. And the thought of making love with Jenny wasn't something that would calm him down. Whatever else had been wrong, that had always been more than right.

Linking his fingers behind his head, Nick stared

at the ceiling. The memory of the first time they made love would be a part of Nick for the rest of his life. Neither of them had planned it, which made it all the more beautiful, all the more meaningful.

He had arrived at her apartment that night to pick her up for a concert. She was late as usual— Jenny never seemed to pay attention to clocks. So while she bathed and dressed, Nick waited.

They had been seeing each other for over a month, but they hadn't even come close to making love. Not that Nick didn't want her. He wanted and needed her, so much it was an ever-present ache in his gut, a constant burning emptiness. It was an emptiness that he couldn't fill. Because Jenny wasn't sending out the right signals.

As stubborn as he was impatient, Nick refused to push her, even though at times he felt like screaming in frustration. She would brush against him or touch him innocently, and he would feel an explosion of desire that threatened to drive him right over the edge.

But he would wait, he thought, fists clenched in frustration. It was too important to him. His goal wasn't simply to possess her body. He needed all of her, her mind and her heart as well. He wouldn't ruin it by rushing her into bed before she was ready.

Restlessly, he paced about the small living room of her apartment. The bedroom door was slightly ajar and in the light of her bedside lamp he caught a glimpse of a framed sketch on the wall. Pushing the door open, he moved closer.

It was only a rough sketch, but Jenny's talent was apparent in every stroke. The subject was also apparent. It was Nick at the bow of the *Reunion*. Why did she have it here on her bedroom wall?

As he studied the sketch, he saw not only pencil lines; he saw intense emotion that came through with vital force. Emotion that pulled at him, causing his muscles to go taut and the palms of his hands to tingle.

Suddenly he felt he was invading Jenny's privacy. He turned to leave and there she was. She stood in the doorway of the bathroom, wrapped in a yellow towel, her long bare legs and slender shoulders gleaming in the lamplight. And on her face was the same emotion he had found in the sketch, and now he recognized it for what it was.

Relief and joy shot through him as he took two steps forward and caught her in his arms, wrapping them around her waist so tightly he lifted her from the floor.

"Oh, Jenny, I've been waiting for this, aching for this since that first day on the boat." His voice was rough as he rained kisses over her beautiful face.

"So have I—oh, Nick, so have I." She was laughing and crying at the same time as she touched him with frantic, trembling hands.

"I ought to strangle you," he muttered huskily. "Why in hell didn't you tell me instead of putting me through the torture of waiting?"

She ducked her head, pressing it to his chest. As the silence drew out, Nick held her chin between his thumb and forefinger, forcing her head up. "Jenny?"

Her gaze met his, and he immediately recognized the confusion and doubt. "I didn't know how," she whispered, her voice breaking on the last pitiful word.

For a moment Nick searched her face in bewilderment, then with dawning amazement. Pulling out of his arms, she moved away from him. Every stiff line of her body told the story. Jenny the lionhearted, his valiant Jenny was embarrassed.

"I feel like a damned fool," she said, her voice gruff as she stared at the wall behind him. The yellow towel lay on the floor, but Jenny seemed totally unconscious of her nudity. "I don't know the first thing about making love," she said emphatically, angrily. She swung her gaze to his face, her eyes pleading. "But I badly want to learn. If you'll teach me, Nick, I promise you won't be sorry."

While she stood there waiting, Jenny finally seemed to notice the expression on his face as he stared at her body. And she saw the flaming desire he couldn't have hidden behind an iron mask. An answering fire blazed in her eyes and her nipples hardened as she drew in a sharp breath.

"You're apologizing?" he said, his voice hoarse, filled with disbelief. "Don't you know? Lord, Jenny, I would love you and want you if you'd slept with the entire Air Force. But this—"

He swallowed heavily, feeling an unfamiliar obstruction in his throat. He stepped closer, his movements awkward, his hand shaking as he reached out to touch her face. So dear, so very dear.

"This is something . . . something so unbelievable—so incredible. You've never wanted anyone enough to let this happen. Only me." He closed his eyes for a brief intense moment. "Only me," he repeated, his voice almost savage. "Do you know what that means?"

She nodded her head frantically. "It means I love you so much I sometimes feel on the edge of insanity."

A deep groan escaped Nick, and as he pulled her back into his arms, the last of the old bonds that had held him prisoner for so long melted away. He felt such an indescribably overwhelming love, such a fierce, obsessive need for her. Jenny said she loved him, but that couldn't begin to describe what he felt for her. She was as necessary to his survival as the very air he breathed.

Hold back, he cautioned himself silently as he felt her trembling in his arms. If she knew, if she even suspected the madness that gripped him when he held her in his arms, it would scare the hell out of her as it would any sane person.

He had to force himself to go slowly, he thought, fighting to contain his emotions. He had to make himself as indispensable to her as she was to him before he allowed her to see the all-consuming depth of his love.

Picking her up gently, he carried her to the bed. He knelt beside her, brushing a lock of dark hair from her face, and looked into her eyes. "Ready, Jenny?" he whispered.

Her eyes gleamed with unshed tears. "For you? Always . . . now . . . forever."

"Forever." He repeated the word, his fingers convulsively tightening in her hair. "That's a promise, Jenny." It wasn't a question. It was a demand, an order he didn't try to disguise with pretty, gentle words.

Her eyes met his fearlessly and without resentment. Slowly she reached up to make an X over her heart. "Cross my heart," she murmured. "Hope to—"

"No!" He wouldn't let her finish. Death had no meaning between them. Nothing could separate them. He would follow her to hell if he had to.

The thought brought the urgency he had tried to suppress surging to the fore. As he threw off his clothes, he felt her gaze like a touch on his body and was overcome by an engulfing need.

Inhaling rapidly, he clenched his teeth in an attempt to gain control. He had to think of Jenny. Leaning over her, he slowly brought the length of his naked body against hers. Only a beginning, but Jenny caught fire from it, moaning as she raised her lips to his shoulder.

"Jenny . . . Jenny . . . Jenny."

He couldn't stop saying her name, using it like a charm as he moved his hungry lips down her throat and then below, pausing at her arching breasts to suck a warm, soft nipple deep into his mouth. As the peak hardened against his stroking tongue, he felt a hot streak of desire shoot to the very center of him. Beautiful, he thought frantically. Beautiful, sweet agony.

He ran an insistent, seeking hand across her stomach. The flesh was smooth, silky, and warm beneath his palm. When he reached the triangle of dark curling hair, he heard her gasp, the sound catching in her throat. A shudder shook him at the thought of giving her pleasure. Threading his fingers through the springy curls, he curved one inward to find her center. Groaning, he searched out the swollen peak and began to stroke it.

Moist and hot, so hot . . . and only for him. The

compulsive thrust of her hips, the hands pressing his mouth to her breast . . . only for him.

Suddenly, coming out of the haze of passion, Nick realized Jenny was crying and his heart jerked in panic.

Moving swiftly, he raised his head and framed her face with his hands, running his eyes over the shadows the lamplight cast on her features. "Jenny?" he said tightly.

"No one told me," she whispered, pulling his head down until her mouth was open against his, open and hungry. "They said it was fun. *Fun.*" She moaned. "No one told me it would be so compelling, so uncontrollable—that I would burn with a fire so sweet I could die from it. No one said that not having you inside me would be like being swallowed up by a monster of emptiness."

When he heard her words and the aching need in her voice, all Nick's careful control was scattered to the wind. A strangled groan escaped him as he quickly covered her body with his.

The natural barrier between them gave easily with a careful thrust, one moment of breathless tension, then she was melting in his arms, wrapping her long, slender legs around him, pulling him close and even closer. He felt breathtaking triumph as he realized she was fighting for him with every movement, with every breath.

The soft light caught the gleam of perspiration on their joined bodies as the thrusts became more and more urgent and liquid fire pulsed through his blood. Then Nick heard a cry from her, so piercingly poignant it brought the sting of tears to his eyes and a swelling joy to his heart.

He felt her muscles spasmodically tighten around

his manhood as she found her final delight. That he could have given this to her, that this wonder of a woman should take such pleasure from his body was enough to send him over the edge in an explosive release.

For a long time they held on to each other as though each were afraid that what they had found would disappear. Nick stroked her damp hair, pausing only when he felt her move beneath his hands.

Her eyes opened languorously, then, drawing in a deep breath, she threw out her arms, her features shining with exhilaration. "Wonderful . . . wonderful . . . wonderful." Grabbing his face between her hands, she leaned down and kissed him hard, then rolled away, wrapping her arms around her waist as she closed her eyes. "*Wonderful.*"

He laughed softly, unable to take his fascinated gaze from her expressive face. "I always knew you had the makings of a wanton."

Yes, he had known, Nick thought. He knew from the way she threw herself wholeheartedly into life that making love with her would be an unforgettable experience. But never in his wildest dreams had he thought he would be transformed by their coming together.

His muscles tightened with growing need as he stared at her. "Come here," he said huskily. Instantly, her eyes darkened, desire causing her breath to quicken as she came eagerly into his arms.

A long time later, while Jenny slept, Nick gazed silently at her face. He knew without a doubt that he had found the missing piece in his life. He had never expected a miracle, but by God, he'd take it. He'd take it with a greedy heart and fight the devil himself for right of possession.

Early in their relationship Nick had admitted that the emotion he felt for Jenny was neither sane nor reasonable. But after loving her, he felt his soul was no longer his own. He wanted to hide this miracle named Jenny away from the world. He wanted to hoard the wonder of her, to hold it tight and never let it go.

But that hadn't been possible, he thought wearily now, his body stiff as he lay on the makeshift bed, staring into the darkness that filled the bungalow. Even before the divorce he had felt her slipping away from him. Now, as he experienced the restless, burning ache, perspiration beaded his forehead, and he kicked himself for his thoughts.

Why had he remembered, tonight of all nights? There had never been anyone like Jenny. Not before, not since. Oh, there had been other women all right. In the weeks after she left there had been quite a few as he sought to exorcise her memory. It hadn't worked. Nick had found a physical release of sorts, but it had served only to point out what was missing.

His failure to find satisfaction with other women had made him angry. He had wanted to smash something because when Jenny left she had taken peace with her. After a while he had come to accept that he would never again find what he had had with Jenny. That was when he had relegated sex to a function, strictly a necessity.

A low sound from the bedroom gradually penetrated Nick's intense retrospection. Lying still, he listened. A few seconds later he heard the sound again. It was a low moan.

Frowning, he sat up, staring at the door that separated him from Jenny. When she moaned again, louder this time, he walked to the door and knocked softly. "Jenny?"

"Go away."

The words were muffled and strained. Pushing the door open, he peered through the darkness. He could barely distinguish her slight form on the bed, but he could see enough to know she had her bare knees drawn up to her stomach as she rocked back and forth.

"What is it?" he asked, moving quickly to the bed. "What's wrong with you?"

"I said go away," she said tightly, as though each word were an effort. "Just let me die with dignity."

In the moonlight he could see the perspiration beading her forehead. Sitting beside her, he fought down panic. "How long were you out in the sun today?"

She groaned, pushing his hand away from her head. "I wore a hat. I'm not stupid."

"Then what in hell is wrong?" he demanded in frustration and concern. "Is it your period? You've never had cramps like this."

"No, it's not . . . it's not my blasted period. Ohhhh," she said, the last word a whimper of pain. "It hurts, Nick. It hurts."

He pulled her against him, feeling helpless as he rocked her like a child. "You've got to talk to me; tell me what's wrong so I can help, Jenny. You've had your appendix out, so it can't be that." Suddenly he swore under his breath. "What did you eat today?" When she simply shook her head and moaned against his shoulder, he grasped her face between his hands. "That's it, isn't it? What did you eat?"

"Sausage, from a street vendor," she whispered hoarsely. "And tamales, and some sweet sticky dessert from a little girl on the corner of the square."

"You idiot!" he said explosively. "You know better than that."

"Don't . . . oh, please, not now. Yell at me tomorrow." She gasped, and held a hand to her mouth. "Right now you'd better get out of my way. I'm going to be sick . . . immediately."

She swayed weakly as she tried to stand, and Nick put his arm around her waist and helped her to the bathroom. Although she tried to push him away, he stayed beside her, holding her while she was violently ill.

When the nausea finally subsided, Nick dampened a washcloth and bathed her face with cool water. He could feel her shivering against him.

But this was Jenny; nothing could keep her down for long. Holding the washcloth to her brow, she glanced at him from the corners of her eye and smiled. "I make it a point to always appear glamorous before ex-husbands," she said with shaky hauteur.

He smiled, relief rushing through him. "Feel better now?"

"Much," she said, moving toward the bedroom. "It's only my dignity that's hurting."

When she was tucked in again, he sat beside her. The tremors still shook her body. He frowned, then reached out and pulled her into his arms.

"You're crazy," he whispered, holding her tightly with the blanket wrapped around her as he leaned against the headboard. "And you deserve every bit of what you've gone through for being so stupid."

"Yes," she murmured dryly, her voice tired, "sympathy, that's just exactly what I need." She glanced up at him through long thick lashes. "What would the bride say if she could see us now?"

"Shut up, Jenny." He inhaled deeply, refusing to let her get to him. "Just try to rest."

Sighing, she cuddled up against him. Nick felt her warmth seep into his body, and for the first time in two years he relaxed completely. Within minutes he fell into a deep, peaceful sleep.

Six

Jenny heard the insistent knocking, but she stubbornly refused to admit the sound into her consciousness. She could have come fully awake with the slightest effort, but it was an effort she was unwilling to make. Instead, she snuggled into the warmth, feeling safe at last.

Safe? As the uncharacteristic and unwelcome feeling penetrated, full awareness hit at last, and Jenny opened her eyes with a frown. Nick was staring at her face, his dark eyes totally devoid of emotion.

Instantly, electric tension grew until it was an almost visible force, filling the space between them with sizzlingly bright emotion. She couldn't bring herself to look away from his eyes. The deep, blank stare seemed to ask questions she didn't know how to answer, questions more forceful than words were being shouted in silence.

The knocking grew louder, and now a new sound

was added, breaking the taut communication, drawing their immediate attention. "Nicky? *Nicky.*"

Jenny met Nick's gaze again. "Does that voice sound vaguely familiar?" she asked slowly.

"Oh, hell," he whispered hoarsely, his expression growing wary as he quickly shifted away from Jenny and scrambled to the edge of the bed.

She tried to stop herself; she bit her lip hard, but it didn't help. Jenny laughed. Rolling over, she buried her face in the pillow. Gulping in air, she calmed down. Then, as she turned and glanced at Nick, the whole thing began again.

As he stood rubbing his palms across his bare chest, Nick stared at her as though she had gone over the edge at last.

"I'm sorry," she gasped helplessly, "but you look like a player in a French farce." Swallowing heavily, she gave him an innocent look. "Should I hide under the bed?"

For a moment he simply glared in exasperation, then, reluctantly, he grinned. "You bitch," he said, chuckling as he pulled her to her feet. Inhaling deeply, he added, "Come on. I may need you to help me explain this."

"Don't look so guilty," she said as they walked toward the door. "We didn't exactly share a night of illicit passion in there. You would have taken care of a dog if it were as sick as I was. Come to think of it," she added thoughtfully, "an ex-wife probably rates lower than a sick dog."

"Just about. I know, I know," he said, shaking his head ruefully. "Logically I can say nothing happened. It must be some kind of genetic guilt."

He pulled the door open, and Elaine, who had

been leaning against it, stumbled in. "Oh, Nick . . . Jenny," she said in relief. "I was afraid the boy in the lobby had made a mistake and you weren't here after all."

Jenny raised an eyebrow in surprise. Elaine had said not one word about her presence in the bungalow or their obvious state of undress. And that wasn't the only strange thing. The neat, calm woman Jenny had met in Fort Worth seemed to have disappeared. As inconceivable as it seemed, Elaine was definitely flustered. Her blond hair was disheveled, and there were streaks of dirt on her pink linen skirt.

Nick took the overnight case from Elaine and led her into the room, closing the door behind her. "What happened? I thought you would be in France by this time."

"I know, darling," the blonde said breathlessly as she brushed back her hair in a nervous gesture. "But suddenly it seemed silly for me to go on alone. When the divorce is final, we can get married here, then fly on to Europe." She glanced at Nick and Jenny, looking unsure of herself. "Would you rather I hadn't come?"

"Don't be silly," Nick said gruffly. "You know I'm glad to see you. I'm just afraid finding a room for you might be a problem. I stayed here—" He broke off to indicate the rumpled cover on the sleeper-sofa.

Jenny swallowed a laugh and murmured in admiration, "Quick thinking."

Glaring at her, Nick continued. "Because there were no rooms available at the hotel."

Elaine bit her lip. "I hadn't thought of that."

She surveyed the bungalow, her gaze lingering hopefully on the bedroom door.

Stepping close to Nick, Jenny hissed, "I will not share my room with the bride, Nick, I won't. I'm not *that* sophisticated."

Obviously at the end of his rope, Nick looked like he was about to commit murder any minute. Jenny didn't want to hang around to see which of his wives he had in mind. "I think," she said, casually moving toward the bedroom, "that now would be a good time for me to get dressed."

Five minutes later, when she came out of the bathroom to find a blouse to wear with the tight white shorts that hugged her slender hips, Nick was in the bedroom zipping his jeans, his feet and chest still bare.

"You took long enough," he muttered, not even noticing her half-dressed state as he headed for the bathroom. "Pitch me my shaving kit, will you?" he called to her as he disappeared around the door.

She dug around in his suitcase and, finding the shaving kit, sailed it toward the open bathroom door. Hearing him yelp, she smiled in satisfaction.

"Damnation, Jenny," he said, keeping his voice low as he stuck his head around the door. "Couldn't you have just handed it to me?"

"You said pitch," she reminded him in a loud whisper, looking over her shoulder as she pulled a vivid blue blouse from the closet.

"Since when have you ever done what I told you to do?"

"Is that what you were looking for—an obedient

wife?" she hissed. "You didn't have much better luck the second time around either. Did you? Elaine is definitely not in France."

His head appeared again around the door. This time he had shaving cream on half his face. "At least she didn't try to kill me first thing in the morning."

"She's probably a night person," Jenny muttered, then said louder, "What kind of welcome was that anyway? You could have at least kissed her."

"That's none of your business." The words were muffled by a towel, but his anger came through loud and clear. "Are you presuming to tell me how to treat my own wife?"

She snorted inelegantly. "Me? I know better. I tried for three years and what did it get me? *Heartache*," she said, pulling on a canvas shoe with unnecessary violence. "That's what it got me."

"Don't give me that," he said, stalking out of the bathroom to glare at her. "You gave as good as you got. You can be a world class bitch with almost no effort."

"And you don't need to put out any effort at all to be a cold-hearted bastard," she said, pulling on her other shoe. "It comes naturally to you." She frowned. "Why are you throwing clothes everywhere?"

"I can't find my sweat socks. Where in hell do socks go when you put them in a suitcase?" he asked, glancing at her in helpless frustration.

"To sock heaven," she said. "Move over. You beat everything, you know that? You've got your life organized down to the smallest detail, but you can never find your socks." Reaching into the pocket at the back of the case, she pulled out the white socks. "And you always put them in the same place when you pack. It must be some kind of mental block," she said, her voice condescendingly kind.

"Oh—go eat a bug," he muttered under his breath.

She gave a shout of surprised laughter. "That's what I like about you, Nick. Always ready with an intelligent, adult comeback."

He grinned as he leaned over to tie his running shoes. "You bring out the worst in me."

"Oh, I don't know," she said, moving to the dresser mirror to apply a thin coat of lipstick. "When you get childish you seem almost human." Swinging around, she inhaled. "I guess it's time to get on with this. Just remember what I said. I won't share a bed with the bride."

"Her name's Elaine, and no one asked you to share your damn bed."

"No," she said softly. "No one asked, but I seem to have done just that last night."

He stared at her and seemed about to say something, when he turned and pulled open the bedroom door.

In the living room Elaine sat on the still-unmade sleeper-sofa. She glanced up slowly as they entered together. "Nothing is going right," she said glumly. "First there was that awful man at the airport in Veracruz. Now there's no place for me to stay."

Nick sat down, putting an arm around her shoulders. "Don't worry. We'll find you a place to stay. What's this about a man in Veracruz?"

She shuddered. "Nicky, he was awful. I tried to find a taxi at the airport, but by the time I had found someone to carry my luggage they had all disappeared. None of the porters spoke English, and I couldn't understand what they were saying. Then this man—this terrible man—approached me and said he would be glad to take me to San Lazaro Ruiz." She looked at Jenny and Nick, her expression indignant. "He knew I thought he was a taxi driver. The beast drove a jeep, and it was open and dusty and all the way from Veracruz he insulted me."

"Insulted you?" Nick asked, his face growing grim.

"He did! He kept calling me a cute chick—me, Nicky, a cute chick."

Jenny bit her lip, trying to assume a sympathetic expression. Nick merely looked nonplussed. "That's all he said?" he asked in confusion.

"That's not half of it. He started calling me princess and telling me how he had been waiting for years to meet me. The . . . terrible beast wouldn't leave me alone. Not even when we finally arrived at the hotel. I was afraid he would follow me to the bungalow—and that's not all."

"You don't mean it," Jenny said, her voice shocked, her eyes sparkling with irrepressible fun. "Not more horror to come?"

"Just wait until you hear," Elaine said indignantly. "About ten miles out of town he suddenly pulled the jeep over to the side of the road and—" She broke off as a violent shudder shook her.

"What happened?" Nick said anxiously. "What did he do to you?"

"He—he picked up a woman and her four children . . . and a *pig*. And, Nicky, the woman gave me the pig to hold!"

It was too much. Nick and Elaine turned to stare as Jenny burst out laughing. "I'm sorry, I'm really sorry," she said, trying to catch her breath. "I don't want to be unsympathetic, but I just got the most vivid picture of the cool, calm woman I met at the reception—holding a *pig*! Lord, I wish Uncle Edgar had been here to see it."

Nick began to chuckle, a deep, rich sound. After a moment Elaine smiled hesitantly. Suddenly, as though she could see her uncle's expression, she giggled, then began to laugh in frank enjoyment.

Leaning weakly against Nick, the blonde glanced at Jenny. "A pig!" she gasped through helpless laughter. "And she handed it to me as though she were giving me a rare treat. Can't you just see Uncle Edgar's face?"

When they heard a knock on the door, Jenny wiped her eyes and grinned at Elaine. "I'll get it. You finish telling Nick about the beast."

A man stood on the other side of the door. He had dark blond hair and was just a half inch taller than Jenny. His ragged, cut-off jeans showed tanned, muscular legs. He looked supremely confident and was cute with a capital C. As Jenny looked him over, he returned the compliment with obvious enjoyment.

Jenny smiled. "Enter the beast."

He grinned back at her. "Only when I'm hungry," he said. "Most of the time I'm Steve McNeal."

"Nicky," Elaine squealed. "He's *here*."

Hearing Elaine's voice, the "cute beast" moved Jenny aside and stepped into the room. His eyes never left the blond woman as he walked steadily toward her.

Abruptly, Nick stepped between them. "Hold on," he said, his voice low and forceful. "My wife says you've been annoying her."

The other man stopped instantly. He met Elaine's gaze, his expression regretful and gently accusing as he smiled at her. "You didn't tell me, princess," he said softly.

After a moment he turned back to Jenny, throwing an arm around her waist. "Well, it looks like it's just you and me, babe."

Jenny chuckled, then, glancing at Nick, she saw his eyes flare violently and caught her breath. Stepping forward, Nick grasped Steve's arm with white-knuckled fingers and forceably turned him toward the door. "Just back off, buster," he growled.

Over his shoulder Steve shot a questioning look toward Jenny. She shrugged and smiled. "I'm his other wife," she explained.

Steve's eyes widened in astonishment. After a moment he shook his head. "The customs must have changed since the last time I was in the States." He looked at Elaine, then at Jenny. "I gotta say I envy you, man. Just one of them would have me delirious."

Jenny grinned, liking this obviously good-natured man. "Let him go, Nick," she said. "I think he's harmless."

"You wound me," Steve said, his expression pained.

"The fact is, Steve," Jenny said, "Nick and I are here to get a divorce so he can marry Elaine."

"That sounds very . . . civilized," Steve said politely. "Sort of a group effort."

Jenny laughed, ignoring the way Nick glowered at her. "Nick just showed up to make sure I did it right—he doesn't trust me," she added. "Elaine came so they could be married when the divorce is final." She glanced at her watch. "Speaking of divorces, I'd better get moving. My appointment with Nuñez is at eleven."

"Matteo Nuñez?" Steve asked.

Jenny nodded. "Do you know him?"

"I know everyone in San Lazaro Ruiz. But I'm afraid you don't have an appointment today."

"Of course I do. Harry arranged—" She broke off as Steve shook his head. "I don't?" she asked warily.

"I'm afraid not," he said sympathetically. "Matt left for Mexico City last night. His daughter ran off with a rock musician. Don't worry, this has happened before. He should be back in a couple of days."

"A couple of days?" Jenny said, her voice stunned. She couldn't let it drag out that long. She had barely made it through one night with Nick; another might destroy her. She had to get the divorce over with and get him out of her life once and for all.

"I'll go to another lawyer," she said, unaware she had spoken aloud.

"Oh, no, you won't," Nick said firmly. "Look what happened last time you pulled a name out of the hat. Harry recommended this guy. We'll wait for him."

Jenny swung around to face him, forgetting the others in the room. "This is crazy, Nick. I want to get it over with. Besides, what are you and the bride going to do—camp out on the beach? There is no room at the inn, remember?"

"Nothing could be simpler," Steve said, startling Jenny and causing Nick to look grim. "Old Nick will stay with me—I've got a place about half a mile down the beach—and the princess can stay here on the couch."

Jenny frowned, glancing at Elaine. "I want my divorce," she said tightly.

"Come on, Jenny," Steve said cheerfully. "This is Mexico. *Mañana* is soon enough. This could be a blessing in disguise. You'll be able to see some of the local sights. We've even got a few Aztec ruins in the area." He smiled coaxingly. "And you won't find a better guide than yours truly in the whole of Mexico."

"No!" Nick and Elaine said at the same time.

Jenny kept a thoughtful gaze on Steve, seeing a way out of the terrible threesome she had been thrown into. "Hold on," she said to the others. "If we're going to be stuck here for several days, I don't intend to sit around staring at you two." Smiling at Steve, she said, "If they don't want to come, that's fine. You can show me around."

Creases dug deeply into Nick's frowning face as he watched Steve watch Jenny. He had recognized the instant empathy between the two, and it made him hate Jenny almost as much as he had hated her the night before, when he had relived the time they had first made love.

He didn't want to spend a second with her that

wasn't absolutely necessary. He wanted her out of his life, out of his thoughts.

"I changed my mind," he said, the abrupt words coming from nowhere. "I'll go too."

Elaine gave Nick a shocked look, then as she moved closer to him, her features grew determined. "If Nick's going, then I will too."

For a moment they simply stared at one another, four stubborn faces giving notice that they were in for the duration.

Seven

Jenny sat with her back against the trunk of a large tree, resting her hands on her knees as she stared at a patch of bright, cloudless sky. Although the denim shorts and cotton knit tank top she wore left most of her body bare, the midday heat was beginning to make her slightly lethargic.

Or maybe it was lack of sleep, she thought, rubbing her head against the rough bark in an unconsciously sensual movement. The night before hadn't been a memorable one. She had wandered around the village for hours, staying out of the way while Elaine rested and Nick reluctantly moved his gear to Steve's house.

Eventually, of course, she had had to go back to the bungalow. When she arrived, the sun was dropping below the horizon, and she had found Nick and Elaine sitting in what seemed a strangely awkward silence. Nick had been predictably furious with her for wandering off without telling anyone; Elaine had more or less ignored Jenny's presence.

The only time the other woman had spoken at all was to argue with genteel vehemence about who would sleep where. Elaine had insisted Jenny take the bed because it was her bungalow, and Jenny had eventually relented simply to gain some peace and quiet. She had spent the next half hour showing Elaine how to open the sofa bed.

Shifting away from the sharp twig under her hip, Jenny let her eyes drift shut. If time continued to pass as slowly as it had so far, she could well be a slobbering idiot by the time Nuñez got back.

Suddenly she tensed and opened her eyes. Nick was standing beside her, looking at her with an indecipherable expression in his eyes.

"Where are the others?" she said, pushing a hand through her already disheveled hair.

"Elaine wanted to take pictures of some flowers for her aunt Luella." He didn't look at her as he lay full length on the grass several feet away. "McNeal went to check on something in the car."

His stiff voice caused her to frown in exasperation. All morning she had been painfully polite to everyone. He could at least make the same effort. "What do you think of the ruins?" she said, keeping her voice bright.

He glanced toward the scattered piles of rock in a small clearing to their right. "It's ruined all right."

"According to Steve, the Aztecs who lived here started something called the Great Pig War," she said, ignoring his disinterest. "The whole population would have been wiped out by fierce warriors from San Lazaro Ruiz if an Aztec god hadn't intervened."

When Nick merely grunted, Jenny abandoned her attempt to be polite and impersonal. "I take it you're not into antiquities these days," she said dryly.

"I like to know what I'm looking at." He didn't bother opening his eyes. "I can see a pile of rocks anywhere."

"Oh, come on, use your imagination," she coaxed. "You still have one, don't you? This was once a thriving village. Throngs of people with colorful costumes milling around the market place— artisans, slaves, priests—"

"Human sacrifices?" he suggested helpfully, opening one eye.

She laughed. "I should have known that if you managed to use your imagination you'd come up with something gory." She gestured toward the clearing. "That little square over there—that could have been the high priest's house. And that long clear space looks like some kind of barracks— maybe the slaves lived there."

"And the big space with the pile of rocks at the end?" he asked, raising up on his elbows.

"It's . . . well—" She frowned, momentarily stumped. "Well, the racquetball club, of course," she said airily.

When he chuckled, she grinned and relaxed against the tree. "You get the idea. People used to live here, part of a civilization we can only imagine. I think it's very exciting. Steve says there are some newly discovered ruins west of San Lazaro Ruiz. Some professors from one of the universities are trying to clear the jungle around it. He thinks he can get us permission from the people in charge to visit the site."

Nick frowned. "When did he tell you this?"

She glanced at him, puzzled by his tone. "I met him in the village late yesterday while the bride was resting to recover from her dreadful ordeal. Why?"

His features tightened. "I don't like the tone of your voice when you talk about Elaine. And I don't like your tone when you talk about McNeal." He moved closer, his eyes suddenly blazing, his vehemence throwing her off balance. "Do you know how often you say 'Steve says'?" He ground the words out derisively. "You sound like an adolescent talking about a movie star."

She felt angry heat flood her face. "If we're going to talk about likes and dislikes, I don't like you interfering in my life. I didn't let you choose my friends for me when we were married. I certainly won't let you do it now."

"Friends? Like hell," he said, his tone sneering.

"Yes, he's a friend," she defended hotly.

"Open your eyes, sweetheart. I've seen the way he watches you." His deep voice was low and threatening. "Come off it, Jenny. What kind of fool do you think I am?"

"I'll bite," she asked inquisitively, "what kind of fool are you?"

He rubbed the palms of his hands over his jeans, then exhaled roughly. "What you and McNeal have going is not my idea of friendship."

She ripped up a handful of grass. "Oh, for sweet Pete's sake," she said in exasperation. "I remind him of home. Steve says I'm typically American and make him realize how much he misses the States."

"'Steve says, Steve says,'" he mimicked explosively. "When he looks at you, the only home he's thinking of has a wall-to-wall bed in it."

"You have a foul mind," she said, her blue eyes flashing. "You take an innocent friendship and turn it into—"

"Innocent, my ass!" he shouted, moving abruptly to loom over her in trembling rage. "The man wants to lick your nipples!"

Startled laughter caught in her throat, bringing on a fit of coughing. "Crude but descriptive," she said, shaking her head in admiration. "Blunt and to the point. You saw all that in his expression? I'm obviously not paying enough attention." She leaned closer until their noses were almost touching. "If you want to talk about relationships, what about you and Polly Purebred? Now, there's a bizarre alliance if I ever saw one. You act more like her uncle than her lover—getting kinky in your old age, Nick?"

His features tightened fiercely, defining every bone in his face. "My relationship with Elaine is none of your damned business," he hissed.

She met his gaze frankly. After a moment she said quietly, "Exactly my point."

His hands clenched and unclenched, and for a moment Jenny wondered if he would hit her. She shouldn't have wondered; Nick was too much in control for that kind of overt anger. After long, tense seconds, his shoulders slumped and he flexed them as though they ached.

"I just don't want to see you get in over your head, Jenny," he said, his expression filled with genuine concern. His gaze roamed restlessly over her features as he reached out to grip her chin and turn her face toward him. "I know you're not promiscuous—you could never be. But you're sensitive, and you're a totally sensual woman," he said, his voice gruff. "I remember—I remember too well."

He stared at her mouth with peculiar intensity. To Jenny it felt like a caress, and her lips began to tingle wildly. The strong fingers on her face gentled, becoming soft. As Jenny looked into his eyes, she forgot everything. She was lost in sable-brown warmth. A deep sensual tension pulled irresistibly at her.

Slowly Nick leaned closer until his lips were only a fraction of an inch away from hers. Jenny was fathoms deep in the spell he had cast with his eyes. It had been so long since she had felt those lips on hers. And Lord, she thought feverishly, she desperately wanted to taste them.

Suddenly he blinked and jerked away, his expression fierce. He lay on his back, not looking at her, his breathing heavy, his arms lying stiffly at his sides as his hands clenched in the grass.

She felt her heart pounding. When she could exert a little control, she said slowly, "An attraction between us is natural. We never had problems in that department." She swallowed heavily. "I mean, it was a part of our lives; we can't just shut it off. But—but it doesn't mean anything."

"Who are you trying to convince? Me or yourself?"

"Oh, for heaven's sake, I'm only trying to help. It's no skin off my nose. I'm not the one with wives coming out my ears," she said, rising to her feet. "If you want to make heavy work of a simple fact of nature, that's your business." She was too emotionally wired to sit any longer, too aware of him to be so close. "I'm going for a walk."

Turning away, she moved quickly, her steps awkward. She didn't care where she went. She knew only that she had to get away from him. Several yards into the jungle she tripped over an exposed root and fell. When she felt a sharp pain in her knee, it seemed like the last straw. She sat where she had fallen, unable or unwilling to stop the hot tears that ran freely down her pale cheeks.

After a moment she heard movement in the foliage and turned her head away, refusing to look up. She should have known he wouldn't leave her in peace. He appeared to have made it his life's work to torment her.

"You're crying," Nick said at last, breaking the tense silence between them. His voice was bewildered, slightly shocked. "You never cry."

"I can cry if I want to," she said with as much aggressive dignity as she could muster between hiccuping sobs.

When Nick stooped beside her, she couldn't help glancing up at him through wet lashes. He looked confused and almost angry as he studied her.

"Yes," she said through tight lips. "I cry, Nick." She ran her fingers across her cheeks and held them out for his inspection. "You see—I cry. Sometimes I cry a lot."

"Why didn't I ever see you cry?" It was more than curiosity. She sensed a strange intensity in him as though the answer were very important. "Why didn't you ever let *me* know when you cried?"

Her laugh was short and unpleasant. "You didn't want to know. I was Jenny, Superwoman. Jenny, with the strength of fifty men." The words caught in her throat. "Only I wasn't," she whispered hoarsely. "I was scared and confused. I wanted to be strong. I wanted to be everything you expected me to be. But after—"

She broke off abruptly. She still couldn't bear to remember. She couldn't bring herself to think of it, much less talk of it. "In the end," she said, drawing in a deep breath, "I knew I couldn't spend the rest of my life pretending. It was debilitating—I was losing myself."

She stood up, looking away from his stunned features. She wanted to hit him. Now, when it was too late, he decided to ask questions. Now, when things were too broken to be mended, he decided he wanted to find out what she was really like.

Swinging around abruptly, she limped back toward the clearing.

"Jenny, wait," he said, running to catch up with her. He grabbed her arm as she reached the tree where they had rested earlier. "You can't just leave it like that. We have to talk. We have to clear this up."

She met his gaze squarely. "Why, Nick?" she asked quietly. "We had a chance to clear it up two years ago and we blew it. We've both made new lives for ourselves." She inhaled shakily. "I think it would be better if we left the past alone from now on. We've hurt each other enough."

He opened his mouth to say something, but at that moment Elaine walked out of the woods with Steve directly behind her. Jenny let out a slow breath of relief. She never thought she'd be so glad to see the bride.

Elaine's pale features were flushed, her hair tousled, and her eyes overly bright and nervously distracted.

"Time to head back." Steve's voice was cheerful. But with her heightened sensitivity, it seemed to Jenny that he, too, was feeling some kind of strong emotion.

On the way back to the car Elaine stumbled, and Steve, who was nearest to her, caught her by the waist. "I can walk by myself," she snapped.

Nick stared at her for a moment, then shook his head as though to clear it. "Do you feel all right, Elaine? You look feverish."

"I wish everyone would just leave me alone!" she said, her voice uncharacteristically fierce.

Jenny glanced at Steve in confusion, but he was already moving to the other side of the jeep.

When they returned to San Lazaro Ruiz, Steve dropped Jenny and Elaine at the bungalow. Then he and Nick went to his house, each man carefully ignoring the other on the way.

Jenny watched Elaine wander around the living room of the cottage, looking a little lost. "Why don't you go rest?" Jenny said at last. "You take the bed this time, and I'll use the couch."

"No," Elaine said, rubbing her hands on her pale yellow slacks. "I've inconvenienced you enough. I'll take the couch."

Jenny sighed in exasperation. "Look, Elaine, we're going to be here together several days. We can't keep up this wary circling. One of us will end up strangling the other." When the other woman refused to meet her gaze, Jenny shrugged. "Suit yourself, but I prefer the couch. Sometimes I don't sleep, and I don't want to disturb you by getting a book or going to the kitchenette."

After a moment Elaine nodded reluctantly and walked into the bedroom. Jenny stared at the closed door for a few seconds, then turned away and threw herself down on the couch. She felt almost as lost as Elaine had looked a moment ago.

What a ridiculous position to be in, she thought with sudden humor. Stuck in a Mexican village with her almost ex-husband's almost new wife.

As quickly as it had come, her humor faded. What had been about to happen between her and Nick today couldn't happen again, not if Jenny were going to maintain what was left of her sanity. She would have to work harder at keeping things casual between them. And no more mention of the past.

She shook her head, trying not to think of the way he had looked when he'd found her crying. What right did he have to look like that—confused and accusing, as though she had deceived him in some way?

What was the use? she thought wearily. She had tried for three years to understand him. It hadn't worked while she was living in the same house with him, why should it work now?

Unbidden memories crowded her brain, causing her to get up and start to pace. Eventually, she stopped and glanced at her watch. She had spent the better part of an hour thinking about not thinking about the past.

If she didn't hurry, she would be late for dinner. And wouldn't Nick just love being able to point out one of her major faults, she thought wryly.

Steve made plans for them for the evening, but Jenny couldn't manage to muster up an ounce of interest. Left to herself, she would be tempted to take a bottle of wine into a dark corner and become a solitary drunk for the night.

With the bride in the next room?

"I don't like roommates," she muttered, walking into the bathroom. "I've never liked roommates. I worked two jobs in college to keep from having a roommate." Quickly stripping off her clothes, she turned on the cold water, closed her eyes tightly, and stepped under the icy stream. She gasped with shock, then clamped her chattering teeth together. "And I especially don't like voluptuous blondes better-than-you-by-a-long-shot debutante roommates."

After showering, she wrapped a towel around her body and, giving one sharp knock on the door, walked into the bedroom. Elaine sat on the bed staring out of the sliding glass doors that led to the patio. She didn't seem to notice Jenny was in the room.

Shrugging, Jenny pulled on her panties and slid her arms through the straps of her bra. As she fumbled with the front clasp, she said, "We don't have much time. They're picking us up at seven-thirty."

Still Elaine didn't turn her head to look at Jenny. When she finally spoke, Jenny barely caught the words.

"I don't want to go."

"Oh, hell," Jenny muttered under her breath in resignation. Elaine sounded miserable, and as much as she wanted to, Jenny could no longer ignore her.

She sat down on the bed beside the slumped figure of the blond woman. "What's wrong?" Jenny said gruffly. "Is there anything I can do?"

Elaine shook her head. "Everything's wrong and, thank you, but I don't think there's anything anyone can do," she said, her voice stiffly polite.

" 'Nobody likes me; everybody hates me; I'm gonna eat some worms,' " Jenny sang softly. When Elaine turned to look at her in blank surprise, Jenny shrugged. "At least I got your attention. Look, you're rich and beautiful—so what are you whining about?"

Instead of losing her temper as Jenny expected, Elaine merely smiled. "You're very blunt. I like that." Her smile faded with a sigh. "I just feel so out of my element here. I don't even know Nicky in this environment. I—"

"Wait," Jenny interrupted shortly. "I think you need someone to talk to and since we're"—she grimaced—"roommates, I guess I'm elected. But unless you want me to throw up on your hand-made Italian shoes, you won't call him Nicky. Nick, or Nicholas, or 'that fishsucking idiot are all just fine, but not *Nicky*."

Elaine giggled at Jenny's disgusted expression. "Okay, I promise."

Jenny nodded in satisfaction. "Now, what were you saying?"

Elaine glanced away. "Not only do I not know Nick anymore, I don't know myself." She paused, a flush spreading across her smooth cheeks. "And I *hate* Steve. He's too casual, too flippant." She bit her lip. "I've never hated anyone in my whole life. I don't like it. It's not me. It's just that I can't deal with his kind of attitude, his kind of person." She turned and met Jenny's eyes. "I envy you."

Jenny almost choked. Elaine had everything. Including Nick. "You're crazy," she said with barely concealed temper. "What on earth is there to envy about me? You want hair that for no good reason at all decides to reach for the sky? You want boobs that wouldn't win a wet-T-shirt contest if Don Rickles were the only other contestant? You want a broken marriage? Take your pick; I'll sell them all to you—real cheap."

"Can I buy a new personality?" Elaine asked softly, effectively dissolving Jenny's outrage.

Jenny shifted in discomfort. "So what's wrong with the one you have?"

Elaine laughed. "You don't have to pretend, Jenny. I know very well what I am. I act like a rich bitch so no one will notice I'm not very bright. I get frustrated because I can't be at ease around men"—she glanced sideways at Jenny—"like you are. I concentrate on trivialities so that I'm not overwhelmed by the important things. How do you do it?" she asked, her voice filled with frustration. "How do you handle men? My mother died only two years ago, but she never told me about anything, especially men." She frowned thoughtfully. "I don't think she knew. But even if she did, we weren't close enough for her to give me motherly advice."

"If she told you the sticky side of the panty liner goes down, it's more advice than I got from my mother," Jenny said dryly.

At Elaine's questioning look, Jenny shrugged. "She left when I was six. I tell everyone my parents died, but the truth is my mother wasn't married. She finally got sick of me and dumped me with her sister. My aunt and uncle were good people, but they had five kids of their own." She rubbed her temple as a tiny, sharp pain struck there.

"But didn't your aunt help you—with growing up and things?"

"I stayed out of the way as much as possible." She laughed shortly. "I guess I was afraid if they noticed me, they'd try to dump me with someone else."

Elaine put her hand on Jenny's arm. "Oh, Jenny, how awful for you."

"It wasn't so bad," she said carelessly. She didn't need pity, especially not from the bride. "I had a place to sleep and lots of good food—no advice about men though." She tilted her head thoughtfully. "In fact, the only information I ever got on that subject was from the bleached-blond receptionist who lived next door."

Elaine's eyes brightened with interest. "What did she tell you?"

"She said that a man didn't exist who could compete with a vibrator," Jenny said blandly. "I don't think that's the kind of information you're looking for."

Elaine gasped, then the two of them fell prey to a fit of laughter, leaning on each other as they giggled like giddy teenagers.

"Thank goodness I was only ten," Jenny said, her voice still unsteady. "I had no idea what she was talking about." Her blue eyes sobered suddenly as a memory—sharp, clear, and breathtaking—took over. "The first time I made love, I knew how wrong she had been . . . and I felt sorry for her."

"Feel sorry for me too," Elaine said. "I'm so ignorant. I'm thirty-one years old, and I've slept with only three men in my whole life."

Well, you're two up on me, Jenny thought dryly. "You don't look thirty-one." It seemed incredible that Jenny was four years younger than the bride. She felt light years older.

"I don't feel thirty-one," Elaine said in disgust. "I feel about fifteen. Making love with those men was . . . nice. But nothing spectacular. I seem to have no deep, intense emotions. It makes me feel like a freak." She sighed. "I use to be terrified that I was a lesbian or something."

Jenny bent down to scratch her toe and managed to put several more inches between herself and the other woman.

Elaine laughed, her eyes gleaming at the carefully blank expression on Jenny's face. "Don't worry, I decided a long time ago that I'm not. But that doesn't help much. I guess there's just something missing in my personality. Nick and I—"

"*No,*" Jenny said, her voice harsh and abrupt. She drew the line at discussing Elaine's sexual relationship with Nick. "I think we should get back to your original question. You asked how I manage to get along with men. I had three boy cousins, and I guess that's why I've never been tongue-tied around men. The thing is, you have to treat them like humans. I know that's hard sometimes, because they rarely act human."

When Elaine laughed, Jenny smiled reluctantly. "But you see what I mean? Don't treat them like *men*—a separate species. Treat them like, well, like overly large people."

Elaine leaned forward to rest her chin on her hand, looking like a female version of *The Thinker*. After a moment Jenny asked, "Why don't you get dressed? We don't have much time." When the other woman still hesitated, Jenny stood and walked to the closet to pull out her dress. "Come on," she said over her shoulder, "anything's better than moping around here. There's too much silence, too much time to think. We both need to get out and have fun. If for no other reason, at least it'll make time pass faster."

Elaine inhaled deeply, then nodded her head reluctantly. She stood and walked toward the bathroom, then stopped abruptly and began to laugh.

"What?" Jenny said, smiling at the infectious laughter. "What is it?"

"This has got to be the strangest situation in the world," she said, shaking her head. "The old wife giving advice to the new."

"Lord, what a revolting thought," Jenny said, her expression appalled. "Maybe I should make fun of the way you dress just to get things back to normal."

"No—no, that's all right," Elaine said warily. "I have a feeling if you and I ever tangled, you would win hands down."

Honey, you've already won the most important prize, Jenny thought, her fingers clenching in the red silk of her dress. Rubbing the unexpected moisture from her cheeks with a rough hand, she continued dressing.

At first glance the small dinner club Steve had chosen was charming, but on closer examination something was slightly off kilter. The dance floor was too large for the size of the club, extending through an open archway onto a wooden terrace, and the dining area much too small for the number of tables crowded into it. The swinging doors from the kitchen were placed so that they interrupted traffic to and from the front door. And behind the trio of musicians was the most godawful mural, depicting, among other things, a pig and an iguana.

When a smiling waiter tripped over a chair and their menus landed on the table with a thud, Steve shrugged. "I'm afraid it's the best place in town," he said apologetically.

"It's . . . different," Jenny said helpfully. "I suppose the food is wonderful."

"W-e-e-e-ll," Steve said, drawing the word out ominously. "It's the best in town. I suggest starting with the avocado—they don't have to cook it."

"The last time Jenny had avocado," Nick said smoothly, keeping his eyes on the menu, "it gave her gas."

It was going to be a wonderful evening, Jenny thought with a sigh. "Now that you've shared that charming anecdote with everyone, Nick, I think I'll order."

"Maybe the sausage," Elaine said. Jenny could tell the other woman was making a determined effort to be natural with Nick and Steve.

"The sausage is okay," Steve said without enthusiasm. "It's made locally—the same stuff they sell in booths on the square."

Jenny choked. "I think I'll pass on the sausage." Glancing up, she caught Nick's gaze on her, his eyes shining with secret amusement.

In the end they all settled on seafood, which Steve assured them was caught right out the back door and, as a result, couldn't possibly be other than fresh. Conversation at dinner was not as awkward as Jenny had expected, perhaps due to the margaritas that, while not the best, were served by the pitcherful throughout the meal.

As they ate, Elaine kept up a flow of casual conversation. Jenny could have kicked both men for being so busy trying to top each other verbally that they didn't even notice the blond woman was acting different.

After dinner, when Elaine and Nick got up to dance, Steve stood and held out his hand to Jenny.

"I'm afraid I don't recognize this song," Jenny said as they moved together around the vast, wooden floor. "Is it Mexican?"

"It's 'Midnight in Moscow,' " he said, grinning.

"Good Lord, how can you tell?"

"They know only four songs, and this is definitely not one of the other three."

"I'm afraid to ask what they are," she said warily.

"I'll tell you anyway, because the others are just as impossible to recognize as this one. The rest of their repertoire consists of 'Muskrat Love,' 'Mamas, Don't Let Your Babies Grow Up to Be Cowboys' and"—he didn't notice how Jenny caught her breath sharply—"the pièce de résistance—'Auld Lang Syne,' played on any and all occasions, regardless of the season."

"What, no Barry Manilow?" she said, forcing herself to relax. "What's the world coming to?"

When Steve laughed and gave her waist a friendly squeeze, Jenny sighed. He's nice, she thought. Nice, and fun to be with. Why couldn't she be attracted to a man like Steve? He was outgoing and took life as it came. And he wasn't so intense, so— He wasn't like Nick, she added silently.

Glancing up, her gaze was caught and held by dark brown eyes from across the room. Immediately her pulse quickened and her flesh tingled.

That's why, she thought dazedly. Life was diabolically ironic. Always good for a laugh, was life, she thought grimly. The only man to make her feel alive was himself stone-cold dead inside.

On the other side of the room, Nick had forgotten the woman in his arms; he didn't hear the music, and the club would have been empty as far as he was concerned. All he could see was Jenny.

Had she worn the red dress deliberately? He had told her once that wearing a red dress was like waving a flag at a bull. His response was automatic. All he wanted was to throw her down and cover her body with his.

And her perfume. It was the scent he had given her their first Christmas together. Damn her, he thought, his lips tight and white. Was she trying to drive him crazy?

Swinging Elaine in an abrupt movement, he turned away from the other couple.

"You and old Nick there seem an odd sort of couple."

Glancing up, Jenny saw that Steve had observed the silent exchange between her and Nick. She felt color come up under her skin. "We not only seem so, we *were* so—which is why we are no longer a couple," she said, making the words light.

"You must have had something going at some point in time. What broke it up?" He studied her face. "Unless you'd rather not talk about it?"

She shrugged. "Why not? It's no big deal, but I'm afraid it's not very interesting. There were a lot of things." She paused, moistening her lips. "We hit a spot of trouble and neither of us could handle it. Instead of bringing us closer together, it pulled us apart. It happens that way sometimes, when people aren't right for each other in the first place, when the love between them is not strong enough." She smiled slightly. "It's all a part of nature. The old ends and the new begins."

"Sometimes the old doesn't really end; it just begins all over again, fresh and new," he suggested gently.

"Dreamer," she scoffed. "You know what happens when you try to bring the dead back to life—you end up with a zombie." She shivered. "Can we please talk about something else?"

Since the music ended just then, there was no need to search for a new topic. Jenny was relieved. Talking about the end of her marriage had left her depressed, and she had had enough of that emotion already to last her a lifetime.

"Isn't the band sweet?" Elaine said as Steve and Jenny reached the table. "Nick and I have a bet on the song they just played. He says it was 'Blame It on the Bossa Nova,' but I think it was definitely 'As Time Goes By.' "

"Close enough," Jenny said, smiling at Steve.

When the band began a new tune, Steve stood. "Dance with me, princess," he said softly.

Elaine stared at him for a moment, shaking her head in a jerky negative movement, then, as though against her will, she stood slowly and followed him onto the dance floor.

Nick met Jenny's eyes and nodded toward the other couples dancing. "Want to give it a try?"

She smiled. "I don't think so. Why don't we stay here and try to be civil to each other? That should use up most of our energy."

He laughed. It was as though that afternoon and the tense moment on the dance floor had never happened. Maybe Nick had made resolutions of his own, Jenny thought.

"It's probably wiser for us to sit it out," he said. "You always ended up dancing on my feet anyway."

"Yes," she agreed sweetly, "and that's because avoiding your feet was like trying to avoid a fleet of submarines in a bathtub."

"Fastest mouth in the West," he murmured, then shook his head. "But I'll forgive—" He broke off, his eyes widening as he listened to the music Jenny had already reluctantly identified as the one they had danced to on their wedding night and again on three consecutive anniversaries. "My Lord, I think I almost recognize this. It's not—"

She nodded, smiling stiffly. "I'm afraid so. We'll probably hear it a lot tonight. Steve says the band knows only four songs."

Although his eyes narrowed momentarily when he heard "Steve says," he met her gaze squarely, then stood slowly, offering her his hand. "One more time, Jenny?"

She swallowed heavily and stood up, walking with him to the edge of the dance floor. When he took her in his arms, she tried not to feel like she was coming home, but it was impossible.

Neither of them spoke as they swayed together in unconsciously sensual movement. Their bodies fit together like two pieces of a puzzle, like they had been specifically formed for each other.

Jenny was tired of fighting. Surely, she thought, surely just this once it wouldn't hurt to give in to the feeling. And that was her last thought. Sensation took over as the penetrating warmth of his body enveloped her in a cocoon that shut out the rest of the world.

When she felt a light breeze on her flushed face, she glanced around with dazed eyes. Although she didn't recall getting there, they had somehow made their way out onto the dimly lit terrace.

As she raised her gaze to Nick's, she knew instantly that it was a mistake. She wasn't the only one caught up in old feelings. His eyes burned with a sable fire that took her breath away and sent heat streaking through her body.

In slow motion his head drew closer and closer until his lips touched hers and clung there. An explosion of desire rocked her to her very foundation. Rising up on her toes, she pressed tightly against him, needing to feel the hard length of his body on hers.

She heard a groan come from deep in his throat, and suddenly the kiss became frantic, his tongue thrusting deeply into her mouth. His hands trembled as they ran over her body hungrily.

"Jenny," he rasped out against her lips, his voice thick with need. "My God, *Jenny*."

His words acted like a match to dynamite. They quivered through her, making her crazy with desire. Then just when she was sure she would die if the kiss ever stopped, a shout of laughter from the club penetrated the sensual fog surrounding them. Jenny opened her eyes, pushing frantically at Nick's chest to break his tight hold on her.

For a moment his eyes remained unfocused in the aftermath of desire, then, as reality settled in, his features stiffened sharply, echoing the shock she herself felt.

She pressed a trembling hand to her mouth. "Dammit, I told you I didn't want to dance," she said, her voice low and fierce with suppressed emotion. "Why did you have to do that?"

"Why did I?" His eyes flared with anger and incredulity as he grasped her arm between hard fingers. "You were somewhere in that clench too."

She had known exactly what she was doing, he thought in grim anger. Those provocative looks and that damned perfume. She had known how easy it would be to slip back into the past. He wanted to strangle her. He wanted—dear heaven, what did he want?

When his fingers on her arm began to tingle crazily, he dropped her arm as though it had burned him and stepped away from her.

Jenny felt wound up tighter than a mainspring. Why did it have to happen? The kiss had reminded her of all she had had to do without for two years, and would have to do without for the rest of her life. And, although she tried to ignore it, she felt guilty. She was beginning to like Elaine. She could even see now why Nick had married her. Guilt and jealousy were an overwhelmingly unpleasant combination.

It was too much, she thought as she felt the sting of tears behind her eyelids.

"Let's go back inside," he said stiffly. "We've done enough damage for one night."

When she didn't move, he stood still for a moment, then stepped closer and swung her around to face him. "Jenny?" he said, his voice softening. Lifting her chin, he turned her face to the moonlight.

She shook her head, releasing it from his grasp. "It's nothing . . . I'm just tired."

"It's not nothing." His voice was low and intense. "You say you cry, but except for the first time we made love, I never saw you cry. You didn't even cry when—"

She knew what he was going to say, and a sound of helpless protest rose in her throat, moving away as she covered her ears with her hands. But it didn't stop him.

"—the baby died."

"*Don't*," she moaned hoarsely as her body was gripped with terrible pain. "I can't . . . I don't want to talk about it."

"No," he said quietly, "you never did."

Even through the pain she heard the quiet agony, the desperate loneliness in his voice. Catching her breath, she took an involuntary step toward him, reaching out to him.

She halted abruptly as Elaine stepped out of the darkness. When she saw Nick and Jenny, her eyes widened in surprise, then she glanced away as though embarrassed.

"I—I have a headache." Her voice was curiously breathless, almost as though she had been running. "It must have been all that sun today."

"Or something," Steve said quietly as he walked up behind Elaine.

Jenny shook her head in confusion. She felt drained and incapable of comprehending her own emotions, much less tackling anyone else's. She simply didn't have the strength to unravel all the underlying tensions around her.

"Yes, I'm ready to go too," she said, moving blindly away from them. She didn't look to see if they followed her. It was all she could do simply to keep walking.

I don't want to get pushy, God, she prayed silently, biting her lip to keep it from trembling. *But do You really know what You're doing with this one?*

• • •

Nick sat with his arms folded on a wicker table that stood on the patio outside the bungalow. He had tried for a while to sleep, but eventually the walls had begun to close in on him. When he had left McNeal's house, he hadn't intended to do more than walk along the beach. He hadn't realized until he saw the bungalow that his feet had guided him there without his conscious consent.

It had surprised him. After what had happened between him and Jenny at the dinner club, he couldn't get her out of his mind.

No, that was wrong, he told himself, frowning up at the brilliant cover of stars. Saying he couldn't get her out of his mind made the thing ordinary, almost a cliché. Nick not only thought about her, he felt her. Now, this minute, as he sat alone in the dark, he felt the smooth warmth of her skin against his. He felt the soft brush of her hair against his face.

It was the same kind of response a man feels when one of his limbs has been amputated. Even though he knows the limb is gone, he still feels it. He doesn't simply imagine it's there; every sense, every natural instinct, tells him it's still there.

That was the way Nick felt about Jenny. Intellectually, he knew she was gone, but his senses continued to send messages to his brain, recognizing her presence.

A sound brought his head around, and there she was. Not an imaginary amputated part of him, but the real live Jenny in her scruffy blue caftan.

"Whoops," she said, her voice slightly chagrined. "Sorry. I didn't know anyone was out here." With an apologetic smile she turned to leave.

"Stay if you want," he said quietly. "You won't bother me."

Liar, he accused himself silently. She bothered the hell out of him, but at least it would be the real Jenny bothering him, and not the phantom presence that haunted him when he was alone.

When she hesitated, he made a short, exasperated sound. "Sit down, Jenny. Sit on the other side of the table. If I have a sudden urge to murder you, the table will slow me down enough for you to get away."

She laughed softly and sat. "If you really decided to murder me, I wouldn't count on anything as flimsy as a table to save me. I would want the Ninth Armored Division at least."

Leaning back in the chair, she propped her feet on another one. "You couldn't sleep either?" she asked lazily.

He shook his head, listening as a light breeze rustled the tops of the palm trees. He could almost count off each individual muscle in his body as it relaxed. The process had begun the minute he saw her standing in the moonlight beside him. It was as though she had brought with her a great, warm blanket of peace and spread it over him.

Now he could sleep, he thought. But the peace was too precious for him to waste a minute of it in sleep. Turning his head to the side, he watched her. She was staring up at the sky as he had done moments earlier. "Stargazing?" he asked, his voice soft in order not to break the spell.

She didn't move her head but kept her face turned upward. "They're not stars," she murmured. "People only think they are. Every one of them is an angel with a candle in a silver holder. You have to watch very closely and when you see your One Particular Angel, she'll wiggle her candle at you."

He nodded judiciously. "Interesting theory. Have you mentioned it to Carl Sagan?"

"Sagan," she said, giving a soft, contemptuous snort. "People listen to him only because he's cute. And the more they listen, the more he knows. He—" She broke off, still looking toward the heavens as she laughed.

"What is it?" he murmured, smiling at the sound of her laughter.

"I've already seen three candles being wiggled at me."

"Somehow that doesn't surprise me." He chuckled softly. "It must take a dozen angels working full time to watch over you."

He turned his head to join her in watching the angels. Did she feel the blanket of peace around them? he wondered. Or was she simply tired of fighting? It didn't matter. Whatever the cause, they had found an island in the middle of the raging ocean, and for a little while they could share the safety and comfort.

For a long time they sat in silence. A four-foot table separated them, but to Nick it didn't exist. They were connected. They were together on one side of the blanket while the rest of the world was on the other side.

"Look, there, just to the left of that cluster of stars," she whispered. "See those six stars? Do you suppose that's the Southern Cross?"

Nick smiled. "I kind of doubt it. You may be able to see it from here, I don't know, but there are only four stars in the Southern Cross and you wouldn't recognize them as a cross unless someone told you."

"Good," she said with satisfaction. "Then that's my cross. I'll call it the Valiant Cross."

"What about those two stars branching out at the bottom?" he said skeptically. "It looks more like a stick figure."

"The Valiant Stick Figure? Somehow that doesn't have the same ring to it."

"Maybe it's the stick figure of an angel," he suggested helpfully. "The Valiant Angel."

"Yes," she breathed. "The Valiant Angel." Without turning her head toward him, she said softly, "Nick, thank you."

Somehow he knew she wasn't thanking him for helping her name her stars. She was acknowledging the small time-out-of-time that they were sharing.

For a long while, even after Jenny finally went back to the bungalow to sleep, Nick stayed where he was, under the blanket of peace she had left behind for him. It was only when the first birds began to announce a new day that he reluctantly rose and walked down the beach, each slow step taking him back to reality.

Eight

The next day they drove forty miles inland to the Aztec ruins Steve had mentioned to Jenny. He had apparently used his abundant charm on the people in charge of the dig, for he had had no trouble gaining permission for them to visit the ruins.

The site was larger than the one they had seen the day before, but it was heavily overgrown. Most of it consisted of unidentifiable mounds and slabs of rock pushing through the foliage. But the main attraction, a small, beautifully preserved step pyramid, had been carefully cleared and made the hot, dusty trip worthwhile.

Jenny managed to separate herself from the others after an hour or so. She wandered about the site, climbing across vine-covered boulders, wondering what they would prove to be when the archeology students finally uncovered them all.

As she explored, she tried to push away the memory of all that had happened the night before. After she had left Nick on the patio, she had asked herself which was worse—the tension and arguments, or the aching sweetness that reminded her of what she had had in the past and would never have again.

She wouldn't think of it. And who, after all, had had more experience at avoiding uncomfortable thoughts than Jenny Valiant Reynolds? Long ago she had learned to quell painful emotions in order to get on with her life.

"No!"

Elaine's voice came from the other side of a large boulder that was all but covered by the encroaching jungle. Grimacing, Jenny moved back into the shadow of the trees. She wasn't ready to see Elaine or Nick yet.

"Not here, not now—"

Jenny heard Elaine's voice clearly; Nick's was only a recognizably male murmur. Jenny thought, wiping a lock of damp hair from her brow, poor Elaine. She sounded almost at the end of her rope. This had not been a fun trip for any of them.

"Don't you understand?" Elaine's voice was rising very close to hysteria. "Yes—yes, dammit, I want you, but—"

Blocking the voices out, Jenny cautiously began to move away. As she put distance between her and the boulder, she still heard the tight murmur of voices but, thank heaven, no longer heard the words. The emotions came through loud and clear. Anger . . . frustration.

Trouble in paradise, she wondered as she pushed aside a low-hanging branch. Why didn't that thought bring her any satisfaction?

Let it go, Jenny, she demanded silently. *It has nothing to do with you anymore. You'll make it. You've always made it. The gremlins have attacked head and heart before, and you've lived through it. Bloody but unbowed . . . well, maybe a little stooped, but you can live with that.*

By the time she returned to the pyramid where the others had gathered, Jenny had regained a measure of peace. One more time Jenny would survive.

"Where have you been?" Nick asked, his dark eyes narrowed with what looked surprisingly like suspicion. Had he sensed her presence on the other side of the boulder during his argument with Elaine?

"Exploring," she said succinctly. "What have you three been doing?"

"We've been exploring too," Elaine said, her eyes and voice overly bright.

Steve sat on a step at the base of the pyramid, wiping his brow with a handkerchief. "Is anyone else as thirsty as I am?"

"Parched," Jenny said emphatically, ignoring the way Nick watched her with quiet intensity. "Why didn't the best guide in Mexico remember to bring cold drinks?"

Steve grinned, rising to his feet. "We passed a store about six miles back. I'll run back and get drinks, and maybe something to snack on. I've made reservations for the night at an inn about ten miles farther inland, but they don't expect us until seven."

"That sounds wonderful," Jenny said in a giant understatement. A night alone—no overwrought roommates, no ex-husbands on the couch, no crowding tension—sounded like heaven on earth.

Steve glanced at them, a brow raised in question. "Anyone want to come with me? At least riding in the jeep circulates some air."

Along with rocks, dust, and assorted insects, Jenny thought, shaking her head emphatically at the same time that Nick said, "No, thanks." Elaine stood for a moment under Steve's inquiring gaze, then without glancing at her three companions, she said quietly, "I think I'll go."

After Steve and Elaine had disappeared into the forest, Jenny decided to climb to the top of the pyramid again, leaving Nick leaning against a slab of rock. She had regained a measure of calm. Being alone with Nick would test her protective shell too much, too soon.

In the center of the front side of the pyramid, a series of small steps divided the huge squares that formed the structure. On these steps, she thought, priests had once walked, followed closely by willing sacrificial victims. In the twentieth century it was not a comfortable thought, but at the time it must have seem absolutely right and absolutely necessary. As she reached the top and looked out over the green canopy of the jungle, Jenny wondered how many of the customs and ideas that seemed right and necessary to modern people would sound appalling to people in the future.

She felt Nick's presence seconds before she heard his step behind her. She stood for a moment, silently gauging her emotional temperature. No tension, she thought in surprise. Was the change in her or in Nick?

"Will the Empire State Building ever look like

this?" he said, his voice low and thoughtful as he echoed her earlier thoughts. "Will people seeing it wonder what amazing ceremonies took place there?"

She smiled. "They'll probably come up with nice pat theories involving priests dressed in three-piece suits who were served by the poor slaves who worked in the mailroom."

His answering chuckle was rich and deep and warm. "And thousands of devout subjects who worshiped in the temple on Wall Street, bowing down in reverence to the stock exchange board."

He glanced at her smiling face and frowned. "Where's your hat?"

She was just beginning to feel the heat on the top of her head. "I left it down there under a tree somewhere."

"Then we'd better get down there under a tree somewhere and find it." He grinned. "I don't know about you, but I'm ready for a rest."

"I'm ready for a cool shower and a pitcher of margaritas, but I guess a rest under a tree will do," she said, allowing him to take her arm as they headed for the steps.

Fifteen minutes later Nick had stretched out under a tree, his eyes closed, his forearms folded beneath his head for a pillow. Jenny sat beside him, resting her chin on her knees as she stared sightlessly at her dusty sandal-shod feet.

After a moment she glanced toward Nick and saw that he had fallen asleep. He must not have gotten any rest last night either, she thought. He looked younger with his features relaxed in sleep.

Sighing, she fought the urge to reach out and stroke his face. She had been a fool to think she could ever stop loving him. And she had been an even bigger fool to hope the love he had once had for her would last forever. There was no anguish in the thought as she gazed at him, only resignation.

Love's not the same anymore, she thought, they just don't make it like they used to. Planned obsolescence was an idea that got around.

The crazy thing about love was that it didn't have to be returned for it to get a permanent hold on the heart. There should be a law against that, she thought, feeling lethargy invade her limbs. People should be allowed only to love people who could love them back.

Stretching out on the grass, she lay on her side, keeping her gaze on Nick's face. She would never be this close to him again.

She would savor this, she thought. She would take the hard angles of his face, the sensuous strength of his lips, the ridiculous length of his dark lashes, and put them all in a mental mason jar and store them on a shelf in her memory. And for the rest of her life, when she needed some joy, when she needed to remember love, she would take out the memory and dust it off, and it would keep her warm for a while.

Gradually her eyes closed and sleep claimed her too.

Jenny wiggled her nose and moved her head away from the tickling, but it came back instantly. At the same time, she felt a sting on her neck and slapped at it. Mosquitoes, she thought drowsily.

Opening her eyes, she found she was curled up next to Nick, her head resting on his shoulder.

Old habits die hard, she thought ruefully. Moving away from him, she shivered. It had grown chilly. When she looked around, she saw that the sun was dropping toward the horizon, casting long shadows. Where on earth were Steve and Elaine?

Reaching out, she shook Nick gently. "Nick . . . Nick, wake up."

"What—what is it?" he mumbled, then opened his eyes and looked at her in surprise. "I fell asleep?" He pushed his hair back. "I must have—" He broke off abruptly at the expression on her face. "What's wrong?" Taking in the shadows around them, he frowned. "Where are Elaine and McNeal?"

She shook her head, her expression fully revealing how worried she felt. "I don't know." She glanced at her watch. "It's just about seven. That means they've been gone almost four hours. What could have happened to them?"

"Damn," he said shortly. "That rattletrap jeep probably decided to fall apart." He met her gaze, his expression softening. "Don't worry about them. McNeal knows this territory, and even though he's an idiot, he'll take care of Elaine. If you want to worry, worry about us. We're going to have to find shelter before it gets dark." He ran a hand through his hair. "Didn't we pass several houses a mile or so before we turned off the main road?"

Jenny nodded. They couldn't really be called houses. They had seen shacks with chickens and children swarming everywhere, but any shelter would look wonderful right now, she decided.

Rising to his feet, Nick pulled her up beside him. "Got your walking shoes on?" he asked, grinning.

Jenny stared in bewilderment. "For a man who's stranded in the Mexican jungle with his estranged wife, you seem suspiciously cheerful."

"Haven't you ever heard of making the best of a bad situation?" he asked, raising one chiseled brow. "Besides, we've just had a nice rest, the sun isn't overhead to fry our brains, and shelter is within reach. What more could a man ask for?"

"Chicken nuggets, an order of fries, and a chocolate shake," she suggested longingly.

His dark eyes gleamed with amusement. "I'm sure we'll be able to buy food from the people in those houses. You'll probably have to settle for tortillas and beans though." He glanced around them. "Let's see, we came in from that direction, so—"

Jenny shook her head. "We came in that way," she said, jerking her head to the left.

"Come on, Jenny," he said, chuckling. "You get lost at Sears. I think you'd better trust me on this one."

When he turned away, she made a face at his back. He sounded so arrogantly sure of himself. Nick was always so positive he was right. What made it even worse, he usually was.

"Nick," she said, bringing him to a halt. "What if Steve and Elaine come after we leave?"

"We'll meet them on the road."

She met his gaze. "I know this is a silly suggestion, but suppose you're wrong and the road is not that way. We could be stumbling around in the jungle for weeks."

"You're right—it's a silly suggestion," he said complacently. "But if it will make you feel better, I'll leave a note."

Taking a receipt from his pocket, he detached a small pen from his keys. Jenny looked away. She had given him the gold pen for his birthday. He always had thoughts about his business when he couldn't find a pen to write them down.

Moments later he walked to the base of the pyramid and placed the note under a rock on the first step. "Satisfied?" he asked.

"No," she said slowly as she examined his patronizing expression, "but if you'll bend over long enough for me to kick you, I will be."

He didn't even bother to hide his laughter as he took her hand and guided her into the forest. As they pushed their way through the foliage, Jenny was positive she hadn't seen any of it earlier. But then, she reasoned, one part of the jungle looked pretty much like the rest.

All the old animosity between them was forgotten as they moved through the thick woods. They had a common goal and worked together to reach it. When they'd gone about half a smile, Nick stopped, frowning as he glanced around.

"It didn't take us this long to get from the road to the site." He stared hard at Jenny. "We obviously chose the wrong way."

She laughed and moved to sit on a rotting log. "What now, Stanley?"

Raising his head, Nick stood perfectly still. He looked like a wild animal honing his senses. After a moment he jerked his head to the right. "This way."

"Why this way?" she said, grabbing his arm to keep up with him.

"Why not?" He sounded remarkably unconcerned. "You can't get more lost than lost."

They hadn't gone a hundred yards when they abruptly broke out of the jungle. In the middle of a clearing, on a small rise, was a house.

A long, stunned silence fell between them. When Jenny finally spoke, the words were slow and filled with disbelief. "We are either dreaming or drunk or we've discovered a new way to get to the Orient," she said, staring at the distinctly curled corners of the storybook house.

Nick smiled. "None of the above. It's real all right," he asid, pulling her toward the house.

"A Japanese house in the middle of the Mexican jungle? That's crazy. Japanese houses are made of paper. Mexican bugs eat everything—including paper."

As they reached the railed wooden porch, Nick took a step up. "It's probably treated," he said, his voice distracted. "Look at the grounds. If they weren't constantly tended, the jungle would have taken over."

He knocked on the wooden doorframe. When there was no response, he rolled up the bamboo curtain and walked inside. Jenny joined him. "No one is living here," he said, indicating the neat austerity of the obviously unused room. "This must be part of a larger estate. Why don't you rest here while I climb that hill behind this place and see if I can spot the main house."

When he moved toward the door, Jenny said, "Nick?" He paused, glancing over his shoulder. "Don't get lost. Please."

He nodded, his eyes warm as he turned and left the room.

Jenny walked out onto the porch and watched as Nick disappeared from sight, then she turned and went back into the house. Inside she examined the room more closely. It was one big open space, with furniture consisting mainly of elegant low tables, carved wooden chests, and some plump cushions on the floor. However, there were partitions that folded out to make two small sleeping alcoves on the right side of the room.

Stepping through the back door, she found herself on a wide terrace overlooking a carefully tended fairyland. The terrace was built around beautifully sculptured miniature gardens. To the left a wooden bridge rose gracefully over a stream that tumbled across rocks and splashed softly into a small shallow pool. The bridge led to a tiny house, a miniature copy of the one she had just left.

As she crossed the bridge, the sound of the water reminded Jenny how hot and sticky she was. She wanted to take off her shoes and wade in the little stream. Maybe later, she thought wistfully as she reached the diminutive house.

When she raised the bamboo covering, she found herself staring at a large sunken tub. Linen towels, soap, and scented oil were displayed on open shelves.

"Even the outhouses are elegant in Japan," she murmured, the sound of her voice startling her.

She felt a little like Goldilocks as she tiptoed into the room. For a second she stood biting her lip, then, glancing guiltily over her shoulder, she reached out and turned on the water.

It worked. As water flowed into the tub, she

shoved her scruples aside and began stripping off her clothes. Carefully lighting several fat candles, she carried them to the wooden platform surrounding the tub.

Then, slowly, to prolong the pleasure, she stepped into the warm water. With a deep sigh she rested her head at the end of the tub. I could stay here for years, she thought dreamily. I could stay here until I get pale and pruny and bloated.

When she found herself nodding off for the third time, she decided it was time to leave. Wrapping a large white towel around her slick body, she grimaced when she looked at her clothes. She couldn't bear the thought of putting the grubby things back on.

Maybe there was something in the house she could wear, she thought, and immediately frowned at the intrusion she was making on the people who owned the house.

"Oh, well," she said, shrugging. "I might as well steal the whole sheep."

Blowing out all the candles but one, she carried it with her. As she stepped onto the wooden porch, she saw movement in the shadows of the garden and tensed.

"Nick," she said, exhaling in relief. "You scared the life out of me. Did you find anything?"

Nick stared at her in silence, taking in the way the candlelight flickered across her shoulders, bare above the towel she had clutched around her. He couldn't let what he was feeling show in his face. There were no memories haunting him now. What he was experiencing at this moment had nothing to do with the past. This was hunger, new and fresh and explosive. He couldn't let her know he wanted her so badly that his body was screaming in outraged frustration.

"No," he said finally, apparently calm. "I followed a trail that's as well tended as the grounds, but I had to turn back when it got dark. I'll check it tomorrow as soon as the sun comes up."

She glanced down at the towel covering her and smiled sheepishly. "I was going to see if I could find something in the house to wear."

"So-o-o," he said, drawing the word out. "While I was out fighting off hordes of vicious, hunger-crazed animals to find a way out of here, you were soaking in a bath." He sniffed the air. "A scented bath," he amended.

"Yup," she said in unconcern, then raised an arched brow. "Vicious, hunger-crazed animals!"

He grinned. "There was a lizard," he offered. "If you're through, I think I'll take my turn in there."

After showing him where the candles and matches were, Jenny returned to the house. In one of the carved chests she found several silk kimonos. Laying aside a white one with embroidered yellow butterflies, she kept digging until she found a larger one for Nick. It was sapphire blue, the fabric heavier than her own, and had a gentle-eyed dragon on the back.

A gentle-eyed dragon, she thought, smiling as she slipped into the white silk. It was perfect for Nick.

When she arrived at the bathhouse, she knocked softly. "Nick, I found you something to wear. Shall I leave it on the porch?"

"No, hand it here." His hand appeared around the bamboo curtain to accept the robe. There was a long moment of silence. "This is it?"

"Ah, come on," she coaxed him. "There's no need for false modesty. You know you've got great legs."

Jenny couldn't make out the words of his grumbled reply, but the disgruntled tone was clear, causing her to chuckle. After a moment she shifted restlessly. "Nick?"

"What?" He didn't sound very receptive.

"Nick, I'm hungry. There's no food in that little paper house." She paused. "I'm getting desperate. Are you sure the walls are treated?"

He laughed, pushing aside the curtain to step onto the porch. "Paper gives you indigestion," he said.

He wore the kimono and carried his clothes over one arm. Jenny let out a long whistle as she stared down at his tanned muscular legs showing beneath the short robe.

In turn, he was examining the kimono she wore. Why did it seem as if he were looking right through the thin silk and exploring the naked flesh beneath? she wondered.

You're just hungry, Jenny, she told herself with mocking humor. And this time it's not for food.

Reaching into the pocket of his slacks, Nick pulled out two rolls of hard candy and handed them to her. She stared in surprise. During their marriage he had always carried candy for her.

Meeting her gaze, he shrugged. "I couldn't seem to break the habit."

"Nick," she breathed in awe as she stared at the candy. "You're wonderful! Two rolls!"

"You're the only woman I know who can make Life Savers sound like a diamond necklace."

"Better," she said, closing her eyes as she savored the lime-flavored sweetness. "Want me to find you a red one?"

They walked toward the house. "I'll take whatever's up next."

Jenny had lit candles and a lantern in the house, and as soon as they were seated on cushions beside a low ebony table, she carefully divided one roll of candy between them.

Scooping hers up in a small pile, she glanced at Nick. "I'll save the other roll for our breakfast."

He snorted in disbelief. "I know you. You'll wait until I'm asleep, then eat the rest."

"Nick!" She gave him an indignant look. "How could you suggest I'd do anything so unscrupulous, so selfish, so—" Breaking off, she glanced at the other roll of candy, then back to his amused eyes. Sighing in regret, she handed it to him. "You'd better keep them."

He grasped her neck to give her an affectionate shake. "Don't trust yourself, do you?" Leaning back, he patted his stomach. "There's nothing like a good meal at the end of a hard day."

Jenny smiled. It was difficult to believe this was really happening. The two of them were sitting together like . . . like friends. She had expected the antagonism to return as soon as their minds were free to allow it. But there was no tension in the room at all.

When her eyelids began to droop, she blinked rapidly, then turned toward the sound of Nick's soft laughter.

"You're sleepy," he said, pulling her to her feet.

She smiled wryly. "I must be feeling my years. Getting lost in a jungle is more tiring than it used to be."

It didn't take long for Nick to pull out the paper partitions that separated the two sleeping alcoves. While Jenny unfolded a woven mat, Nick put out the candles and the lantern, and then there was only the moonlight filtering in in muted silver streaks through the paper walls.

As she stretched out beside the partition that separated her from Nick, she heard him doing the same in the other room. For a long time she stared at the patterns, drawn in gentle chiaroscuro on the walls.

"Nick," she whispered, her voice softly merging with the silence.

"Hmm?" His low reply came immediately, telling her she hadn't disturbed his sleep.

The sound of his voice in the warm darkness was curiously intimate and somehow comforting. With the thin divider between them, they were close enough to feel the togetherness but separate enough to be free of embarrassment. This must be how a confessional feels, she thought.

"Suddenly I'm not sleepy," she murmured.

He shifted on his mat. "Me neither."

"Want to talk?"

"Sure." His voice came back to her quiet and low. "What do you want to talk about?"

After a moment she whispered, "I don't know. I was thinking this was like a confessional. My cousin Myrna used to have friends over, and I would listen to them lying in bed telling their deepest, darkest secrets. They would stay up all night giggling. I guess it was because in the dark you can't see a person's eyes—no accusation, no embarrassment." She laughed softly. "Maybe we should take turns telling all those things that nobody in the world knows."

"This sounds interesting. What sins have you been indulging in lately?"

She searched her mind, riffling through the dozens of minor sins and vices. Suddenly she smiled. "As a matter of fact, I've had a secret vice for years and I've never told anyone."

"Tell," he urged, his husky voice filled with indulgent amusement. "Tell all, Jenny."

"Don't get all excited. It's just a tiny little vice. You know all those ten-pound tomes I used to carry around with me?"

"You were determined to improve your mind."

"I read them all right, and some of them I even enjoyed, but those were, as you said, for my mind. When I needed to feel, I read something else."

"Oh?" The word was filled with deliberate sexual overtones.

"Not that kind of feeling," she whispered indignantly. She hesitated, drawing out his suspense. "I read love stories."

"God, no!" he said in mock horror. "And all these years you've managed to hide it from decent people. Strange," he said thoughtfully, "it never showed on your face."

"Oh, shut up," she said, laughing. "I always hid them from you because I was afraid you would make fun of them."

Silence fell between them, then, exhaling audibly, he said, "I would never have done that, Jenny."

She stared at the ceiling. Maybe he wouldn't have. She had had so many fears back then.

"I enjoyed them," she continued. "I still do, when I have time to read them. They're . . . secure. You always know that the people will be happy. When life gets a little shaky, it's nice to go to a place where things always turn out right."

She gurgled with laughter as another thought struck her.

"What?" he said, and she heard the smile in his voice. "What are you thinking of?"

She moved next to the screen, and as though he read her mind, he moved closer. If the paper wall hadn't been between them, her lips would have been next to his ears.

"In the books," she said, her voice low and confidential, "they're always making love on white fur rugs and on coffee tables and on satin comforters. I always want to say, 'Okay, who's going to clean up this mess?' "

Suddenly they were giggling like the teenagers she had described earlier. Nick was laughing so hard, Jenny could feel the wall shaking between them.

"And," she gasped, holding her side, "no one *ever* goes to get a washcloth."

That set him off again Jenny was afraid the wall wouldn't hold up. When the laughter gradually died away, they lay in companionable silence.

Turning her head toward his outlined shape, she said quietly, "You were like a romantic hero."

"I don't know how to take that. Does that mean I wasn't real to you?"

"Maybe, I don't know. Mostly it was because you were so . . . so out of the ordinary. I never felt like I measured up. Those women in romantic novels, they would have been right for you. They're all lacy French silk bras. I've always been cotton and practical."

"I wish I had known, Jenny," he said. "I let you down in more ways than I care to remember."

Jenny couldn't believe what she was hearing. "No," she said, her voice shocked. "It was the other way around. I was the one who fell short. Even before—" She drew in a deep, calming breath. "Long before we separated I could see the gap growing between us. I knew there was something you needed that I couldn't give you."

"That gap meant there was also something you needed that I couldn't give to you." He sounded tired.

Silence fell again. This time it wasn't quite so comfortable. Jenny had begun to wonder if he had fallen asleep, when he began to speak.

"I guess it's my turn to confess."

Nick listened to the sound of his own voice. He wasn't even trying for lightness. He knew Jenny could hear the intensity, but he didn't care. It was well past time for her to know.

"I want to tell you what happened to me when I met you," he said. "I should have told you a long time ago."

He paused, not waiting for a response, just trying to make sure the words would come out—the right words this time.

"That first day on the boat seemed like magic to me. I guess I'll always see it that way. Until that day I thought I was satisfied with the way my life was. I'd lived the way I was for a long time, and it seemed to fit my idea of what was right. Then you came along and suddenly I saw that I hadn't simply established a nice, sane pattern for myself. I had given up. I had stopped fighting for the best life had to offer. You made all the joy, all the wonder of life available to me. But more than that, you made it easy. It was as if you were saying, 'Come on, stupid, it's there for you. All you have to do is open you hands and take it.' And I did. With you beside me I took it all."

He shifted restlessly. "But you can't stop the habits of a lifetime that easily, Jenny. I began to wonder what my life would be like if you ever decided to leave me. I guess that's when the whole thing got out of control. My obsession for you grew until it scared the hell out of me. I was afraid even to let you out of my sight. And I knew that if it scared me, it would terrify you. That's why I hid it from you. That's why—"

He stopped, exhaling roughly. "No, that's not completely honest. I have to be honest now, Jenny—with you and with myself. That was only part of the reason I hid what I was feeling. A big part was that I resented the hold you had on me. I told myself only a weak, spineless fool would be so totally dependent on another human being. I was so busy fighting my obsession for you that I forgot to live our life together, our marriage. I consciously put distance between us. Because that's the way I had always handled things. It was only after you left that I stepped back to look at what had happened, at what I had done. It was too late to change things, but it didn't stop me from having regrets. After a while I had to stop thinking about it. The guilt and pain were eating me up. I got rid of everything that made me think of you." He paused. "Everything except that key chain pen. And if someone mentioned your name, I got mad as hell, because it ripped me up to hear it."

He closed his eyes, his hands clenched beside

him, and for a long time he couldn't speak. Then, finally, he inhaled slowly and turned his face toward her. "The worst part is that I know if I had been more open with you, you could have come to me when—when you were hurting. I'm sorry about that, Jenny." The words were a rough, pain-filled whisper.

Jenny lay in the darkness, feeling physically and emotionally numb. What had begun as a light-hearted conversation had suddenly turned into something overwhelming. She had never expected that kind of honesty from him. She didn't know if she could handle that kind of honesty.

She rubbed her throbbing temples. Maybe she couldn't handle it, but she couldn't ignore it either. It would be nothing short of cruelty to let him go on bearing all the blame.

Rolling over, she turned her back to him. What she had to say was easier that way. "I lied to you, Nick." The words rushed out of her. "I told you both my parents died. I never knew who my father was. I don't suppose even my mother knew who he was. She never loved me—I knew that all along—but it still was a shock when she left me with her sister. That was when I was six. By then I was used to being without love. All I wanted was security. The whole time I was growing up I was waiting for my aunt and uncle to tell me I couldn't live with them anymore. That never happened, because they were good people. I—I wasn't a very lovable person back then; I can see that now. But it still hurt knowing no one was there for me. When I met you and you seemed to love me, I went around holding my breath, afraid it was just a dream. The night we got married, when I tried to break it off with you, I had been dragging up of all kinds of stupid excuses why it was wrong, but deep down I was thinking, 'This man can't love me. Why should he? He's so beautiful, so wonderful. Why would someone like that love me?' "

She turned toward him, her lips trembling. "The whole time we were married I was preparing for it to end." She inhaled shakily. "So you see, it wasn't only you. We both made mistakes. We have to share the blame for ruining our marriage."

"I—" His voice sounded choked. "I wish I had known how lonely you were."

He raised his hand and placed it on the screen. For a moment Jenny simply stared at it, a dark, strong shape outlined in moonlight. Then slowly she raised a hand and pressed it to his.

She heard him release his breath in an audible sigh. After a moment he rolled onto his back. Jenny could almost feel him relax, as though he had been tense for a long time.

It was a long time later when Jenny spoke again. "Nick," she murmured. "Do you feel lighter somehow?"

"You feel it too?" he asked, his low voice filled with wonder. "I feel—not quite so old. Only that doesn't really describe it either."

She laughed softly. "We need one of your sesquipedalian friends here right now to tell us the proper word to use."

"Not really," he said dryly. "Words—communication—is important, but sometimes the feelings are all that are necessary."

"I don't think Mr. Malcolm would agree with you."

"Malcolm? I don't remember any Malcolm."

"Sure you do," she said, rolling over to face his shadow. "Remember the New Year's Eve party that Harry and Sharon gave, the one where the fat redhead fell in the pool?"

He chuckled. "Who could forget? Sharon had a fit when she saw the red dye floating on the top of her pool. But what does that have to do with Malcolm?"

"That's where I met him, but you already knew him. At least he said you knew him. He backed me in a corner around eleven and started filling me in on the ins and outs of etymology. I remember wishing you could hear him because he used such big words to tell me about such small words that I couldn't understand a thing he was saying."

She laughed huskily, then yawned as drowsiness finally began to hit her. "And to make it worse, his ears wiggled when he talked," she murmured. "After about fifteen minutes I looked around for you. You were standing by the sliding glass doors talking to a petite older woman." She let her eyelids drift down, but continued talking. "It was as though you knew I was looking for you, because at that moment you glanced up, and I remember I shivered because you had that look in your eyes—"

She broke off abruptly, her eyes opening wide as she realized what she was about to say.

"What look?" he asked. When the silence drew out, he asked again. "Jenny, what look was in my eyes?"

For a moment she simply lay there in the dark, then as though she no longer had control of her words, she began to speak. "It was always the same look and it always had the same effect on me. It didn't matter where we were—in the middle of a crowd or completely alone. You would turn around and I would see that 'wanting you' look in your eyes . . . and I would go crazy for you."

She could feel the heat sweeping through her veins as she remembered how many times it had happened. And it had never failed to drive her wild. She had never, before or since, experienced anything like it.

Caught up as she was in the memory, it was a moment before she sensed she was no longer alone. When she glanced toward the end of the partition, she felt every muscle tighten.

Nick was standing there, his naked flesh reflecting the pale moonlight. She couldn't move; she couldn't breathe as she stared, mesmerized by the rugged beauty that had once been so much a part of her life.

"Look at my eyes, Jenny."

The words were a husky whisper that seemed a part of the warm night air surrounding her. Lifting her gaze, she did as he asked, and her breath caught in her throat.

"Is this the look?" he asked as he knelt beside her.

Nine

Jenny stared at Nick, her heart pounding in her ears. He knelt there beside her with his hands at his sides. The fluid grace of his arrow-straight body, unyielding and still, defined honesty—a sculpture in silver-dipped copper. And as she stared, the night between them grew heavy with silent waiting.

"Is this the look?" he repeated, and now his voice was hoarse with some strong emotion.

Her gaze never left his as she gave a single, jerky nod. When he raised his arms to her, Jenny went into them instinctively, irresistibly drawn to the unleashed power of their combined need.

Like magic, the kimono slid away and then it was flesh against flesh; hard strength against yielding softness; man against woman, as it was meant to be from the beginning of time. Together they lit a fire that wouldn't be contained.

She felt the sweet possession of his touch spread through her limbs like liquid sunshine. When he cupped her buttocks in his large hands and raised her up, molding her lower body against his, a sound rose in her throat, a soft aching sigh of pleasure.

They sank to the mat, not as two separate people, but as a single unit, a unit that is able to function only when the two parts are in place.

Suddenly a small, whimpering moan escaped her. She pulled away from him, scooting back into the corner. Closing her eyes tightly, she listened to the hectic sound of their breathing.

Nick exhaled a shuddering breath and reached out to lift her chin, silently demanding that she look at him. When she opened her eyes, he said quietly, "What's wrong, Jenny?"

She moistened her lips. "Elaine."

"You remembered Elaine?"

"Yes." Her throat was so tight, the single syllable was painful.

A long moment of tense silence passed. She tried to read the expression in his eyes, but his mind was closed to her.

"And that was enough?" he asked slowly. "That was enough to make you say no to this?" He reached out to cup her breast, watching the rounded flesh swell beneath his touch, watching her eyes flame with desire. He let his hand drop. "Maybe you're right." The low, calmly spoken words reached her ears as an accusation. "If it's not so urgent, if the feeling isn't so powerful that ten wives couldn't stop you, then it doesn't come anywhere near what I feel."

He paused, drawing a hand across his face. "I don't think I can settle for anything else."

His movements were tired and old as he rose to

his feet and turned away from her. Jenny bit her
lower lip until she drew blood. She wanted to
plead with him, to stop him. She wanted to tell
him her reluctance had nothing to do with Elaine.
It was Nick himself. If he loved her, nothing—not
time or space or the loss of heaven—could keep
her out of his arms.

She shivered as the coldness began to seep into
her bones, spreading quickly to settle around her
heart. She clenched her fingers into tight fists as
rage welled up inside her. Sweet Jesus, she thought
in desperation, didn't she deserve one night?
Elaine would have him for the rest of her life; why
couldn't Jenny have him just for this night?

"Nick." Jenny didn't recognize her own voice.
The word was too rough, too frantic to have come
from her.

As she came up on her knees to follow him, to
beg if necessary, she opened her eyes and found
he had never left the room. He was staring at her
with the same feverish need in his eyes that she
knew was in her own.

"One more time, Jenny?"

The hoarsely whispered words exploded in her
brain, freeing years of repressed longing, leaving
her helpless to resist.

"Yes, please—yes, oh, yes," she breathed.

Reaching out, he brought her hands to his body,
pressing them against him. "Touch me, Jenny.
Touch me and watch me go crazy."

Jenny's urgent hands returned to places she
had found only in aching dreams over the past
two years. Dear, familiar places—the strong ten-
dons of his neck, the shallows above his breast-
bone, the ridged muscles of his stomach rippling

under her fingers, the long, hard line of his thigh. As she touched him, she felt every muscle of his taut body shake. Jenny watched . . . and died a little from the deep pleasure she was giving him.

When she slid her fingers over and around the throbbing heat between his thighs, a groan rose from deep in his throat and he pulled her down to the mat. "I need to feel all of you," he whispered urgently. "Every inch of you touching every inch of me. This is what's haunted me for two years, your face . . . your body . . . your voice whispering in my ear. Night after night I'd wake up in a cold sweat from the dreams."

She felt his heart beating against her as it raced out of control. Her mouth opened to his, meeting the slick roughness of his tongue with her own. The hands on her breasts, the hard lips on hers demanded something of her that she didn't even consider denying.

"Now, Nick," she rasped out, her hips rubbing urgently against his as she tried to assuage the aching need. "Please—now. I can't stand anymore. I've got to have you in me."

"Yes, Jenny, *now*."

Her body had become supersensitized, and she felt the full hot length of him as he eased inside her. He filled her completely. He filled her with strength, with mind-spinning delight, and she laughed in unadulterated relief.

For a long moment they simply lay together, reveling in the incredible rightness of it. Then he began to move slowly, prolonging their ecstasy.

But when she wrapped her long legs around him, urging him on, he went wild and the thrusts became frantic, dynamically energetic. She felt as if she'd been freed from slavery. She felt as if she were flying.

It had never been so intense between them, she thought, her mind dazzled as she rose to meet him. In the past his movements had been carefully controlled. This time Nick had lost all restraint.

He suddenly grabbed her buttocks with both hands and rolled over, settling her astride him. Weak with desire, her head drooped forward, causing her hair to make a dark curtain around them. He reached out with a trembling hand to push the strands on each side behind her ears.

"I couldn't see you in the shadows," he said. "I need you up there with the moonlight on your face. I want to watch you. I want to see your face when it happens for you."

The words struck her to the core, sending her out of her mind with desire. She dug her fingers into his biceps, unaware of the marks she made there. Leaning back, she rocked against him, then, as her need grew, she began to move. Nick had always been the giver—now Jenny was giving to him. Rippling sensations spread like wildfire through her body, and she was being consumed by it.

As she felt the gathering intensity, she threw her head back. Her eyes were open, huge, seeing whirling visions of wonder. Her lips parted and each panting breath seared her. Then her body turned to liquid as pleasure shuddered through her, shaking loose and setting free all her old conceptions of ecstasy.

From somewhere far away, but reaching her clearly, she heard his cry of triumph. Then she sank slowly, weightlessly, to his chest, his arms holding her secure, assuring her that she wouldn't fall off the mountain on whose heights she had seen eternity.

When the bells stopped ringing wildly in her ears, she didn't move her head but raised one hand blindly to touch his face. She felt his lips on her fingers, kissing each one as they moved across his mouth.

It felt so wonderful, lying there. Her knees were still drawn up, her toes moving gently across his thighs.

"Jenny?" he murmured against her pinky as he stroked her hair.

"Mmmm?" The sound was filled with languid contentment.

"Who's going to get the washcloth?"

She giggled helplessly, burying her face in the curling hair that spread across his chest. She could feel him rocking beneath her with laughter.

"Oh, Nick . . . Nick, what did we do?" she moaned, moving her face restlessly against him.

"Don't." His fingers tightened in her hair. "Don't regret it. Whatever happens in the future, this was right. Didn't you feel it? It was a healing, Jenny. It was wiping out the hurt. We owed ourselves that much."

"Yes," she sighed. "Yes, we deserved that much."

He moved with her in his arms until she was lying beside him, her head cradled on his shoulder. Nothing more needed to be said. They had said it all with their bodies. With her eyes closed, Jenny listened as his breathing slowed and he drifted off to sleep.

All through the night she listened and she

watched. Every minute with him felt precious and she didn't want to lose even one of them to sleep.

The first faint rays of the sun were filtering into the room when Nick opened his eyes and saw her there, still watching. Glancing down, he moved his hand down her hip and across the smooth flesh of her stomach.

When she caught her breath, he raised his gaze to hers. Slowly his dark eyes filled with a bittersweet sadness. "I think this time you would regret it," he whispered huskily.

"I'm afraid so." She was unable to keep the wistful longing from her voice.

He sighed heavily, resting his head on her breasts. His fingers tightened at her waist for just a fraction of a second as he brushed his lips across her bare flesh. Then without another word he moved back slightly.

Squatting beside her, he brushed the hair from her cheek. "We need to talk, Jenny. There are things I need to explain. But not now. Later, when we get back to San Lazaro Ruiz."

Jenny nodded. She didn't understand, but it wasn't necessary. The night had taught her many things. And one was to take each moment as it came, one at a time.

Half an hour later she groaned deeply, frowning at Nick as she placed one hand on the small of her back and stretched tentatively. "I don't think Japanese mats were made for American backs," she grumbled. "All those cute little electronic things they manufacture can't make up for the fact that not one of them can produce a decent bed."

They had spent fifteen minutes wiping out the evidence of their visit and now stood on the porch, discussing what their best course of action was.

Nick chuckled as he watched her twisting this way and that to work out the kinks in her back. "Are you sure it was the bed?" he asked, raising one brow suggestively.

She smiled. She couldn't remember a time in all the years she had known him that she felt as close to him as she did this morning. It was something very special, something she would treasure for the rest of her life.

Leaning toward him, one hand holding the wooden rail, she poked him with a not-so-gentle finger. "There are things that work out kinks and things that put them in. But I suppose at your age it's hard to tell the difference."

"Is that what you were doing last night?" he asked, smiling. "Working out the kinks?" With an arm around her waist he settled her against him. "Yes, I guess it was at that." He inhaled deeply. "Look at it, Jenny. Have you ever seen such a beautiful morning?"

Not in two years, she thought, reveling in the comfort of his strong body beside her.

Suddenly, without a single trumpet to warn them, a figure stepped out of the forest and walked toward them, a hand raised in greeting. Jenny moved away from Nick, and together they watched the end of their idyll approaching.

"I thought I'd find you here," Steve said as he drew near the house.

"Fancy meeting you here," Jenny said, keeping her voice light. "Did you have to go to Houston for the cold drinks?"

"Where's Elaine?" Nick asked, his voice toneless.

Steve met his gaze. "She's fine, Nick."

When Nick nodded, Steve turned back to Jenny.

"A funny thing happened on the way back to the ruins," he said sheepishly. "The jeep, bless it's tired little heart, decided to take a long nap." He glanced behind them at the house. "Looks like you two had better beds than the princess and I."

"I wouldn't bet on it," Jenny said dryly. "At least the jeep has padded seats."

"That's the only plus, believe me." He reached into his pocket. "I thought you might be needing these about now," he said, handing Jenny two bags of peanuts.

"Food!" she exclaimed, turning to Nick. "Look, Nick, a veritable feast." When she tossed him a bag, their gazes met and he smiled, teasing her, bringing back memories of the night before.

Steve, his foot propped on the wooden rail, looked from one of them to the other, but his expression revealed none of his thoughts. "I left the jeep in Valdez's driveway—about a quarter of a mile back. Elaine's waiting there."

"Valdez?" Nick asked as the three of them began to walk away from the house.

"He owns this place." Steve grinned broadly. "I bet you thought you had stepped through the looking glass when you saw the house."

"I loved it," Jenny said softly. "But why would anyone build something like this, here of all places?"

"About ten years ago he was engaged to a Japanese girl—he built the house for her so she wouldn't get homesick. The day before the wedding she ran off with her father's gardener. Valdez keeps the place just exactly like it was, but as far as I know, no one has ever stayed there." He glanced at them. "Until now."

As they reached the beginning of the jungle forest, Jenny paused and looked back over her shoulder, running her gaze over the beautiful little house, sending it a silent good-bye.

All those year, she thought. Valdez had spent all those years wanting someone he couldn't have.

She let out a shaky breath. One moment at a time, she told herself. Take one moment at a time.

Jenny woke abruptly, her eyes wide open in the darkness. What had awakened her? she wondered as she rolled onto her side.

Even though she had stayed awake the night before, it had taken her a long time to get to sleep on the sofa bed. An exhilaration she hadn't chosen to examine had been singing through her blood.

The four of them had returned ot San Lazaro Ruiz in time for lunch, but Jenny had been the only one with an appetite. Elaine had been abrupt to the point of rudeness, refusing to speak to Nick even though he had pressed her with unusual force. She had pleaded a migraine headache and hadn't left her room for the rest of the day.

At that moment Jenny heard voices filled with hushed intensity coming from the bedroom. Instantly she knew what had awakened her. When she heard the bed creak loudly, she stiffened, pressing her hands to her ears.

Why now? she thought, drawing in a harsh breath. Why had Nick come to Elaine's room tonight? Had their night together panicked him? Had he gone to Elaine to prove to himself that his night with her meant nothing?

Slowly the tension eased out of her and she relaxed with a sigh. As though he had spoken the words himself, Jenny knew that whatever was taking place in the bedroom, Nick was not making love to Elaine. Maybe someday in the future he would resume his physical relationship with the woman, but not tonight. Not so soon after they had held each other, needing to wipe out the hurt of the past.

She was wide awake now and knew she couldn't stay where she was, trying not to listen. She slid off the bed, grabbing her robe as she moved toward the door.

Outside, she headed instinctively for the moonlit beach. As she walked, her bare feet left light footprints in the sand.

Why are you lighter than air tonight, Jenny? She smiled, raising her face to the moonlight. *Silly woman,* she answered herself silently, *because Nick made love to you. Because no matter what happened in the past or will happen in the future, for one night you were just exactly what he needed.*

Gradually, the sound of the waves and the warm night air reached out to her, and there was no thought, merely sensation.

Nick stood under a palm tree, watching Jenny walk slowly up the beach toward him. Her robe was open, the ties trailing behind her, her long legs showing from beneath the worn cotton shirt.

Sweet heaven, she's beautiful, he thought. A bohemian goddess. A rumpled angel who was caught flying a little too close to the earth. His pulse raced with the pure joy of looking at her.

When Jenny heard the steps beside her, she

didn't have to look up to know who it was. She had been specially attuned to the essence of Nick for too many years.

She glanced at him from the corners of her eyes. "Hi, cutie," she said, her voice husky. "Haven't we met somewhere?"

He chuckled. "You're awfully cocky tonight."

"Yes, yes, I am." Throwing out her arms, she whirled around and around before him on the sand, then came to a swaying stop when she got dizzy.

He caught her arms, pulling her up straight. "What have you been drinking?" His eyes were warmly amused as he stared at her upturned face.

"Moonlight and fairy dew," she said immediately. "Not available in bars or clubs. Do you want some?"

"It may be just exactly what I need tonight," he murmured, then, with an arm around her shoulder, they began to walk.

They walked side by side in silence for about a hundred yards, then turned around and began to walk back toward the bungalow.

"We've done a lot of talking lately," he murmured, then laughed softly. "More than we did in the whole three years of our marriage, as a matter of fact. At least we've said more. Because this time we were really communicating."

"Yes."

She reached up to hold the large hand on her shoulder. It felt warm and safe in the shelter of his arm. Strangely, the thought of him bringing her safety no longer bothered her.

"There's one subject that we've avoided." He paused, meeting her eyes. "I think we should talk about it now."

Jenny didn't have to ask what the subject was. She knew. Without hesitation, without regret, she nodded. "Yes, it's time."

She stared ahead for a moment, but she had no need to search for words. The words had been waiting for over two years to be set free.

"I had known for a long time things were wrong between us," she began slowly. "But I refused to recognize it. You remember how adept I am at pushing the bad to the back of my mind and focusing on the good. I thought if I didn't acknowledge the distance was there, maybe it would disappear. Then when I found out I was pregnant, it seemed like a prayer that I hadn't even known I was praying was answered. Your baby. I never dreamed anything so wonderful was possible for me. Beyond that was the hope that the baby would bring us closer, give us back what we had had in those months before we got married. When I told you—"

She stopped, closing her eyes as she smiled at the memory of how happy they had been. "You seemed to come back to me. For months I went around in a fuzzy pink haze—making plans, redecorating, buying ridiculous toys. I felt the baby growing inside me—I felt it move—I came to know it as a living person.

"Then it died." She said the words flatly, without emotion. "I think if I had miscarried early in my pregnancy, it wouldn't have been quite so devastating. It would have hurt, but it wouldn't have left the lingering emptiness that having a still-born child left. And when I finally worked through the pain, I looked up and found out that somewhere along the way I had lost you again. I couldn't handle it," she said with a small, almost careless shrug.

"You explained why the distance was there originally, but this was different. I depended on you too completely. You had the ability to make my life heaven or hell back then. I found out I wasn't strong enough to endure the hell." She reached down to pick up a bit of shell and hurl it into the waves, dislodging his arm as she moved. "It took a while for me to admit that it was over. All those scenes, all those terrible quarrels—" She smiled, shaking her head at the person she had once been. "It was my way of fighting the inevitable. I thought if I could just make you look at me and *see* me, then maybe we would have a chance."

She glanced up at him, but his face was turned away from her. "I also resented your calmness. That's something I didn't admit until after I left. I guess I wanted to see you throw something or pound your fists on the wall. Anything would have been better than acting as though the baby had never existed. But when I finally got your attention—that day I went to your office and screamed at you in front of the whole board of directors—that was the day I knew I would have to leave. You looked at me at last and there was no love in your eyes."

Somewhere along the way Jenny's false calm had left her, and her face was unnaturally pale in the moonlight. The memory brought a strangling tightness to her throat. "There was only blame in your eyes when you looked at me. *It wasn't my fault that the baby died*," she whispered hoarsely. "It wasn't my fault."

Nick stiffened beside her, jerking his head back

as though she had struck him. He grasped her arm, swinging her around to face him.

"You thought that?" he rasped out through tight white lips. "You thought I blamed you?"

She searched his harsh features. Her hand trembled as she brushed it across her face in confusion. "Didn't you? Didn't you, Nick?"

"Dammit, no!" His laugh was short and ugly. Dropping her arm, he leaned his head back, staring up at the star-filled sky. "How ironic, how hellishly ironic."

He straightened his shoulders and met her eyes again. "When you told me about the baby, I was over the moon. I couldn't think of anything more wonderful than my child growing inside you." His strong lips twisted in a self-mocking grimace. "I also thought it was a perfect way to keep you tied to me forever. I've already told you about the obsession I was fighting, so you can see I was already handicapped. Then gradually, as I watched you planning for the baby and saw that you were happier than you had been in months—happier than I could make you—I began to worry." He paused. "It sounds so crazy now, *so damned insane.*"

When the silence between them drew out, she whispered anxiously, "Can you tell me? Please, I'd like to know."

He smiled slightly, sadly. "I think I have to." Dropping to the sand, he pulled her down beside him. "When I saw your happiness, I began to wonder if, when the baby came, I would be on the outside again. It seemed to me, in my insanity, that you were transferring the love that should have been mine to the baby. And if I felt the loneliness before the baby was born, what would it be like afterward?" He inhaled deeply, as though fighting to draw the air into his lungs. "That was when I began—"

When he broke off, running a shaky hand across his face and moistening his dry lips, Jenny suddenly realized just how painful the memories were for him, how they had each suffered alone. She felt a terrible emptiness inside her.

"That was when I began to resent the baby," he continued as though drawing up his last ounce of strength. "To—to regret your pregnancy." The stark agony in his eyes leaped out at her. "You see, Jenny, the blame you saw in my eyes wasn't for you. It was for me. When we lost the baby, I felt as though I'd killed it myself." The words came through clenched teeth as he swayed slightly. "I hated myself for that. I still do."

"*No!*" She moaned as she scrambled to her knees to pull his head to her breasts. "No, love, hush, don't do this to yourself." She rocked back and forth, holding him against her. "I should have been there to help you—I should have seen. It's all right, Nick—I promise it's all right."

It was a long time before their shared tears completed the final cleansing. Together they stayed on the moonlit beach, their arms wrapped around each other tightly. When the darkness softened in the east with a faint penciling of light on the underside of a cloud, Jenny and Nick rose slowly to their feet.

"It's finally over," she said quietly, smiling up at him.

"Yes, it's over," Nick confirmed, automatically understanding the simple statement. The deep wounds had at long last been cauterized.

With a sigh she reached up to stroke his face. "Good night, Nick."

"Good night, Jenny."

He watched her walk away, feeling a tightness in his chest, a deep frown creasing his features. Why had it sounded so much like good-bye?

He didn't move when he heard other, heavier footsteps approaching, but seconds later Steve stood beside him on the beach. For a while neither of them spoke, then Nick said, "Got another of those?" indicating with a nod the cigarette Steve held in his fingers.

"You don't smoke."

"I didn't yesterday; I won't tomorrow, but right now I need a cigarette—unless you've got a bottle of tequila on you."

Steve gave a short laugh, tossing a half-empty pack to Nick. Minutes passed as they smoked in silence, then Steve flexed his shoulders. "Lord, what a mess," he said, his frustration almost comical.

Nick didn't look at him. Instead, he stared sightlessly at the beginning of a brilliant sunrise. "It'll work out," he said slowly. "It has to." Then he turned and walked away.

Ten

When Jenny walked back into the bungalow, the light was on in the bedroom and she knew immediately that something was wrong. The sounds coming from the next room weren't the gentle, elegant tears of a debutante, they were the wrenching sobs of a frightened child.

Slowly she raised her eyes to the ceiling. "Can't I even have a traumatic experience in peace?" she asked in frustration.

Sighing, she walked to the bedroom and pushed open the door. "Elaine," she said softly, "what's wrong?"

The only answer was a deep moan. Jenny walked to the bed and sat down beside the figure huddled under the sheets. She stared at her for a moment, searching for a possible reason for Elaine's anguish.

"Are you upset because Nick isn't paying enough attention to you?" Jenny asked reluctantly. "I know there has been . . . an atmosphere between him and me lately—I can explain that."

"It's not Nick!" Elaine burst out, sitting up to rub her eyes. "It's Steve. Jenny—" She paused, her eyes wide with horror. "Jenny, he wants me to marry him."

"Oh, you know how Steve is always kidding around. He probably—"

"We've made love." The confession was bold, almost a boast. "Twice. *Ohhhh*." Turning, she flung herself back on the rumpled bed. "It was so wonderful . . . and I just want to *die*." She drew in a deep, shuddering breath. "I love him, Jenny," she said softly, sadly.

Jenny stared in disbelief. "You and Steve? That was Steve in here tonight? And you've—"

Elaine sat up, pushing back her hair. "Yes, we've made love. And I don't feel guilty about it." Her reddened eyes didn't make her any less haughty as she glared at Jenny. "You don't have to sound so outraged. What exactly were you and Nick doing last night?"

Jenny shrugged her shoulders in irritation, chagrined that she and Nick had been so obvious. "That was different. That was leftover lust . . . clearing up the past—oh, I don't know. Give me a minute. This has confused me a little."

She should have known. If she hadn't been so involved with Nick, with her own emotions, Jenny would have known. All those times that Elaine and Steve popped up together. All the secret eye-play and tension between them.

And if Elaine married Steve, Jenny's way to Nick was clear.

Now the truth comes out, she thought wryly. It had been in the back of her mind even before she and Nick had made love. By hook or crook, by fair means or foul, Jenny wanted Nick. And Elaine was handing him to her on a silver platter.

But what about what Nick wants? a nagging voice asked.

Jenny's first instinct was to tell Elaine to get the hell away from Nick. He deserved to be loved totally, heart and soul, the way she loved him. That's what he deserved, but what did he need?

Between them she and Nick had cleared up the past. So where did that leave them? Maybe the bad memories were the only thing that had kept Nick bound to Jenny. Now that all the pain, all the regret, had been swept away, was there anything left?

He had not said a word about the future, and he hadn't said a word about love. There was still the giant difference in their personalities, something that would never change. He had told her at the reception that he needed order, that he needed a normal life. Even if she put all her effort into it, she could never be normal and orderly. The only way he could overlook her defects was if he loved her. He would have to be totally out of his mind in love with her, she thought sadly.

Glancing up, she saw her image in the mirror. *Is this a woman who drives men wild? Is this the face that launched a thousand ships?*

"Not even a leaky rowboat," she muttered with regret.

"What?" Elaine stared at her in bewilderment.

"Nothing," Jenny said, shaking her head. "It was nothing. Let's talk about this logically. You're not being fair to Nick. You made promises to him. Besides, you can't marry Steve," she told her firmly.

"You're not cut out for love in a hut. No designer clothes, no servants, no imported caviar."

"I don't need those things," Elaine said, but Jenny could tell she was weakening. If the loss of material possessions could sway Elaine, her love was not very strong.

"Maybe not, but think of your family. How are you going to tell them your marriage to Nick was a fake? How are you going to tell them you're going to marry a man you've known only for a couple of days, a man with no visible means of support." Jenny saw Elaine's eyes cloud with doubt, and she went in for the kill. "Your father and Uncle Edgar would come down on you like the ten plagues of Egypt."

When Elaine shivered, Jenny continued in a more gentle voice. "Nick needs you, Elaine. You're sane and normal." She grimaced. "He didn't find those qualities in his first wife."

"Sometimes," Elaine said softly, "I've thought he was still in love with you. I've seen him watching you."

Jenny felt her heart leap, then she shook her head. "We simply needed to straighten out the past. We've done that. Now it's time to get on with the future."

"I—I guess you're right, Jenny." She lay back on the bed, her voice weary as she threw her arm over her eyes. "I don't want to let Nick down. I'll have to do some thinking, won't I?"

Jenny stood up and walked toward the door. She had done the right thing, she told herself. Then she told herself again . . . and again. But the instant she switched out the light and went into the sitting room, she thought, *What in hell have I done?*

At noon the next day, Jenny, Elaine, and Nick sat at a table in the patio restaurant of the hotel. Jenny pushed the food around on her plate, avoiding Nick's eyes while Elaine made no pretence at eating and avoided the eyes of both her companions.

The silence was finally broken when Steve walked up to the table, swinging a chair around to sit on it backward. "Good morning, all," he said, not even bothering to glance at Nick and Jenny as he stared at Elaine.

The blonde drew in a quick breath, shifting restlessly in her chair. The tension between Elaine and Steve was not hidden now; it was all out in the open.

Jenny glanced quickly at Nick to gauge his reaction. But he was turned away from her, his narrowed eyes trained on Steve and Elaine as though he were waiting for something important.

"There was a message for you at the desk, Jenny," Steve said, his gaze never leaving Elaine's face. "Matt's back. He can see you today at four."

Jenny placed her napkin on the table with a hand that shook only a little bit. "So—this is finally it."

When she felt Nick's hand on hers, she looked up slowly. Then suddenly Steve rose to his feet, kicking the chair away in a startlingly abrupt movement.

"You've got to make up your mind now, princess," he said. His voice was more intense than

Jenny had ever heard it. "We won't have fancy cars and diamonds. We won't fly around the world to chase the seasons." His expression gentled as she met his gaze. "But we will have more love than you ever imagined," he whispered huskily.

Jenny could almost feel the effect the words had on Elaine. Leaning forward, she said urgently, "What about our talk last night? Don't be a fool. You said you would stick by Nick. You said—"

When Nick's fingers tightened painfully on hers, Jenny broke off and glanced at him hesitantly from the corners of her eye.

"You idiot," he said gently. He smiled and the look in his eyes brought heat to her face, confusing her, pushing every thought from her head.

Elaine came abruptly to her feet. "I'm sorry— Nick, Jenny. I didn't mean for it to happen, but it did. That's what makes it so special. No matter what you said last night, Jenny, I belong with Steve. For the first time in my life I'm complete. I'm real."

Jenny jumped to her feet. "But—"

"Shut up, Jenny." Nick stood beside her with his arm around her waist as he looked at Elaine. "If he makes you happy, go for it." He smiled. "I'm glad for you. You deserve this."

Steve didn't wait for any more discussion. Clasping Elaine's hand in his, he pulled her away from the table and out of Nick's life.

As they reached the edge of the patio, Steve glanced over his shoulder, meeting Nick's gaze. "Good luck," he said, grinning.

"I don't understand," Jenny muttered, shaking her head vehemently. "I don't understand any of this. I think you've all gone mad."

Thoughts and emotions were pushing at her from all directions. But she had no chance to sort them out, for at that moment Nick grasped her chin and raised her face to his.

"Let's go back to the bungalow, Jenny," he murmured huskily.

Jenny stared at him wide-eyed. It was obvious he wasn't asking her to share afternoon tea with him. The look in his eyes was familiar. Familiar and so welcome. Jenny had never been able to resist that look.

As soon as they were in the bedroom and she was in his arms, the desire to straighten out what was happening was lost to another desire. Jenny knew all she needed to know—she was back where she belonged.

Their slow, lazy lovemaking, so different from the night in the Japanese house, filled her senses to overflowing. Jenny reveled in it, she breathed it in, she absorbed him into her system.

It was late in the afternoon when Jenny and Nick walked arm in arm along the beach, leaving the sunbathers behind them.

"You know," she said. "I haven't seen your lip twitch or you scratch your palm in two days."

He smiled. "So?"

"So nothing—just making an observation." She glanced up at him. "Are you very upset about Elaine?"

He chuckled, shaking his head. "Sometimes you are so dense," he said affectionately.

Her eyes flared. "And sometimes you—"

He placed one finger on her lips, silencing her. "When Elaine and I met, I was almost as lonely as the day I met you. And so was she. We were drawn together because of that. I knew I would never fall in love again." If he felt Jenny stiffen beside him, he didn't acknowledge it. He merely continued speaking in a steady tone. "Elaine had emotional problems. She convinced herself—and me—that she would never have a normal love life." He inhaled slowly. "Elaine wanted children. I wanted to give back what I felt I had taken away." He stared at the ocean. "We were open about the fact that we didn't love each other, but we thought we could have a good life together."

He grinned suddenly. "Then a blue-eyed tornado swept in and disrupted all our sane, orderly plans. Thank God." The words were heartfelt. "At first I thought there was no need for you to know all this. Then when I realized there was very definitely a need, I couldn't say anything because Elaine had asked me not to. I wanted to clear up things with her before I talked to you."

He met her eyes. "So now you see why I'm not upset. I thought, no, I hoped, something was happening between Elaine and McNeal, but she avoided me, refused to talk to me." He laughed. "It was the most frustrating thing I've ever had to deal with—except for you of course."

Jenny didn't know what to say. She had suspected Nick was not deeply involved with Elaine, but she had still thought that the other woman was what Nick needed. Now he was all but telling her he was relieved that Elaine and Steve had gotten together.

Brilliant bits of happiness were nudging at her, trying to get into her heart. With Nick staring at her so steadfastly, so expectantly, she didn't know where to look; she didn't know what to think.

Glancing at her watch, she moistened her lips nervously. "It's almost time for my appointment with Nuñez," she said helplessly.

He lifted her chin gently. "Did you think I made love to you just now because I was upset about Elaine?"

"I—I don't know what I thought," she admitted. "I guess I considered it a possibility."

He smiled, the sweetness of it driving her crazy. "And did you make love with me to comfort me?"

Jenny almost said yes, but his eyes wouldn't let her lie. "No," she said tightly, almost belligerently. "It didn't take me long to forget all about the bride."

Jenny wanted to kick him for looking so unconscionably pleased with himself. Releasing her chin, he stooped to pick up a handful of sand. "Did you have your heart set on seeing Nuñez, Jenny?"

Jenny felt her heart jerk then pick up again in a hectic beat. She brushed the hair from her forehead. "No—no, I guess not."

The silence drew out between them. She was ready to scream, when he finally spoke again.

"Jenny?"

"Yes?"

"When in our marriage did you stop loving me?"

She gave a sharp, harsh laugh. "You don't ask for much, do you?"

"From you?" He turned and met her eyes. "Only everything, Jenny."

The expression on his face sent heat and exhilaration racing through her. "Actually," she whispered, "I never did stop. If I never saw you again, I would still love you until I die."

His breath caught in his throat and he pulled

her into his arms, swinging her around and around until they were both out of breath. And over and over again he said the words she had been aching to hear. Nick loved her. Nick really loved her.

Frowning slightly, she reached up to touch his face. "I'm still irrational and impulsive, Nick." She grimaced. "I think you ought to know before we go any further."

"I hadn't noticed," he said, teasing her with his laughing eyes.

"I'm serious—listen to me," she said urgently. She had to know that this time it would be all right. "I'm still a cockeyed optimist. I still believe in angels and find something good in everything I see."

"Show me, Jenny," he said huskily. The vulnerability in his face brought hasty tears to her eyes. "Show me the angels, help me see the good." He pressed her close to his chest. "You keep everything, Jenny. You never throw anything away. You put things in boxes and on shelves and keep them forever." His arms tightened around her. "Keep me too, Jenny."

And she did. Jenny kept him in her arms and close to her heart for the forever she had once promised him.

THE EDITOR'S CORNER

Thanks for all your wonderful cards and letters telling us how glad you are that we've added two LOVESWEPTS to our monthly publishing list. Obviously, it's quite a lot of additional work, and, so, we are especially glad to welcome Kate Hartson as our new senior editor. Kate has been in publishing for more than seven years and has edited many different kinds of works, but in the last few years she has devoted a great deal of her time to romance fiction and has edited almost one hundred love stories. Kate is as fine a person as she is an editor, and we are delighted to have her on our team.

You have six delicious treats to anticipate next month from Peggy Webb, Sandra Brown, Joan Elliott Pickart, Kay Hooper, Charlotte Hughes, and Iris Johansen. I probably don't need to say more than those six names to make you eager to get at the books—but I had so much fun working on them that it would be virtually impossible for me to restrain myself from sharing my enthusiasm with you.

Peggy Webb presents a heartrending love story in **PRIVATE LIVES**, LOVESWEPT #216. John Riley is a man whose brilliant singing career has left him somewhat burned out; Sam Jones is an enchanting woman who blunders into his rural retreat and brings more sunshine and fresh tickling breezes into his life than he could get in the great outdoors. This moving romance is a bit of a departure into more serious emotional writing for Peggy, though she doesn't leave her characteristic humor behind. Her lovers are wonderful, and we think their healing power on each other will leave you feeling marvelous long after you've finished reading about their **PRIVATE LIVES**.

FANTA C, Sandra Brown's LOVESWEPT #217, is a sheer delight. On the surface heroine Elizabeth Burke seems to be a bit straitlaced, but her occupation—and her daydreams—reveal her to be a sensual and romantic lady. She owns and operates a boutique in a large hotel called Fantasy, where she sells such items as silk lingerie and seductive perfumes. It is in her rich and powerful fantasy life that she expresses her real self . . . until neighbor Thad Randolph comes to her rescue, dares to fulfill her secret dreams, and turns fantasy into reality. A keeper, if there ever was one!

LUCKY PENNY by Joan Elliott Pickart is LOVESWEPT #218 and another real winner from this talented and prolific author. Penelope Chapman is a complicated woman with a wealth of passion and sweet sympathy beneath her successful exterior. Cabe Malone is a man who secretly yearns for a woman to cherish and build a life with. They meet when Cabe finds her weeping in the house he is building . . . and his very protective instinct is aroused. Soon, though, Penny must flee, and Cabe sets off in hot pursuit. A breathlessly exciting chase ensues, and you'll cheer when these two lovable people capture each other.

News Flash! Kay Hooper is being held hostage by a band of

(continued)

dangerous, sexy men, and they aren't going to let her go until she's finished telling the love story of each and every one of them. And aren't we lucky? Fasten your seatbelts, because with **RAFFERTY'S WIFE,** LOVESWEPT #219, Kay is going to sweep you away on another glorious caper. This time that sneaky Hagen has Rafferty Lewis and Sarah Cavell in his clutches. He's assigned them the roles of husband and wife on an undercover assignment that takes them to an island paradise in the midst of revolution. But Rafferty and Sarah are falling deeply, hopelessly in love, and their madness for each other is almost as desperate as the job they have to do. Watch out for Sereno . . . and don't think that just because Raven and Josh are on their honeymoon they are going to be out of the romantic action. It's only fair to tell you that Kay has created a marvelous series for you. Look next for **ZACH's LAW,** then **THE FALL OF LUCAS KENDRICK,** then . . . well, more on this from me next month!

Exciting, evocative, and *really original* aptly describe, LOVESWEPT #220, **STRAIGHT SHOOTIN' LADY** by Charlotte Hughes. When Maribeth Bradford comes to the bank in her small town to interview with its handsome new president for a job, she walks into a robbery in progress. Suddenly, she finds herself bound back-to-back with devastatingly attractive Edward Spears and locked with him in a dark closet. . . . And that's just the beginning of a great love story between a devoted small-town gal and a city slicker with a lot of adjustments to make. We think you're going to be utterly charmed by this wonderful romance.

THE SPELLBINDER, LOVESWEPT #221, by Iris Johansen delivers precisely what the title promises—a true spellbinder of a love story. Brody Devlin can hypnotize an audience as easily as he can overwhelm a woman with his virile good looks. Sacha Lorion is a waif with wild gypsy beauty who has a claim on Brody. Her past is dark, mysterious, dangerous . . . and when her life is threatened, Brody vows to protect her. Both of them swiftly learn that they must belong to one another body and soul . . . 'til death do them part. This is a magnificent story full of force and fire.

Enjoy!

Sincerely,

Carolyn Nichols

Carolyn Nichols
  Editor

LOVESWEPT
Bantam Books, Inc.
666 Fifth Avenue
New York, NY 10103

Imagine yourself Loveswept ®

SHEER MADNESS

SHEER BRILLIANCE

SHEER ROMANCE

SHEER PASSION

SHEER COLOR

All it takes is a little imagination and more Pazazz.

The first Delaney trilogy

Heirs to a great dynasty, the Delaney brothers were united by blood, united by devotion to their rugged land . . . and known far and wide as

THE SHAMROCK TRINITY

Bantam's bestselling LOVESWEPT romance line built its reputation on quality and innovation. Now, a remarkable and unique event in romance publishing comes from the same source: THE SHAMROCK TRINITY, three daringly original novels written by three of the most successful women's romance writers today. Kay Hooper, Iris Johansen, and Fayrene Preston have created a trio of books that are dynamite love stories bursting with strong, fascinating male and female characters, deeply sensual love scenes, the humor for which LOVESWEPT is famous, and a deliciously fresh approach to romance writing.

THE SHAMROCK TRINITY—Burke, York, and Rafe: Powerful men . . . rakes and charmers . . . they needed only love to make their lives complete.

☐ *RAFE, THE MAVERICK by Kay Hooper*

Rafe Delaney was a heartbreaker whose ebony eyes held laughing devils and whose lilting voice could charm any lady—or any horse—until a stallion named Diablo left him in the dust. It took Maggie O'Riley to work her magic on the impossible horse . . . and on his bold owner. Maggie's grace and strength made Rafe yearn to share the raw beauty of his land with her, to teach her the exquisite pleasure of yielding to the heat inside her. Maggie was stirred by Rafe's passion, but would his reputation and her ambition keep their kindred spirits apart?   (21846 • $2.75)

LOVESWEPT

☐ YORK, THE RENEGADE by Iris Johansen

Some men were made to fight dragons, Sierra Smith thought when she first met York Delaney. The rebel brother had roamed the world for years before calling the rough mining town of Hell's Bluff home. Now, the spirited young woman who'd penetrated this renegade's paradise had awakened a savage and tender possessiveness in York: something he never expected to find in himself. Sierra had known loneliness and isolation too—enough to realize that York's restlessness had only to do with finding a place to belong. Could she convince him that love was such a place, that the refuge he'd always sought was in her arms?

(21847 • $2.75)

☐ BURKE, THE KINGPIN by Fayrene Preston

Cara Winston appeared as a fantasy, racing on horseback to catch the day's last light—her silver hair glistening, her dress the color of the Arizona sunset . . . and Burke Delaney wanted her. She was on his horse, on his land: she would have to belong to him too. But Cara was quicksilver, impossible to hold, a wild creature whose scent was midnight flowers and sweet grass. Burke had always taken what he wanted, by willing it or fighting for it; Cara cherished her freedom and refused to believe his love would last. Could he make her see he'd captured her to have and hold forever?

(21848 • $2.75)